Here and Nowhere Else

By Dr. Sopna Nair

OrangeBooks Publication

Smriti Nagar, Bhilai, Chhattisgarh - 490020

Website: **www.orangebooks.in**

© Copyright, 2022, Author

All rights reserved. No part of this book may be reproduced, stored in a retrieval system, or transmitted, in any form by any means, electronic, mechanical, magnetic, optical, chemical, manual, photocopying, recording or otherwise, without the prior written consent of its writer.

First Edition, 2022

ISBN: 978-93-5621-264-0

Price: Rs.270.00

The opinions/ contents expressed in this book are solely of the author and do not represent the opinions/ standings/ thoughts of OrangeBooks.

Printed in India

Here and nowhere else

"I'm here in this fleeting moment, nowhere else, just here"

Dr. Sopna Nair

OrangeBooks Publication
www.orangebooks.in

Acknowledgement

To Almighty God and the entire universe for all the blessings bestowed on me.

To my dad, *S K Nair* for loving me enough to let me be myself.

To my friend and my love, *Prem* without your support, this book might have still remained a dream.

To my life, love and everything - my kids, *Nachu* and *Navvu*. *Nachu,* you really supported and helped a lot, beyond your age for this book.

To my dear friend, *Ms. Muskan* for all the lovely inputs and support during the editing of this book.

To an awesome friend, *Mr. Sajeev Kumarapuram* for the extremely beautiful cover page design and for all the support with the great guidelines, whenever I was stuck.

To *Prof. Pfeifer, Mrs. Ute Pfeifer, Mr. Guido Noelle* and *Mr. Karsten Veith* for all the constant support you all rendered me over the years in my professional life.

To my lifelines, my dearies *Sobha, Subha, Preethika, Divya, Sivakala* and for our *SSPeeDSS* gang. I am so lucky to have you all in my life.

To *Haritha* and *Savitha* and our timeless friendship, which got kicked off when we were just teenagers.

To my special friends *Manoj* and *Bharat* and the bracing you offer for keeping my spirit high.

To my *Classy* group of friends who are competing with each other to prove who can fix each other's crowns better. A special thanks to *Smija, Divya* and *SaiPriya* for being there always lending your ears to me.

To my *Hotties - Dimple, Linda, Preetha, Rini, Sreeja* and *Shruthi*. For all the warmth and laughter, we share together.

To the two simple yet lovely people in my life. My *Deedi* (sister) and *Mummy* (mother-in-law) who are always there for me with your support and love.

To the lovely young couple *Eldo* and *Neenu* for doting over me and my family.

To my exuberant friends *Jitesh* and *Zeno*.

To the lovely relationships I cherish with *Delfin, Hashim, Alex Uncle* and many more on the list.

To my PT, *Rahul Umarane* for all the kind motivation and changes you brought out in my life.

To my *dear mother*, I have no words to say how grateful I am to you always. I miss you like anything!

Preface

This has been a journey of varied sorts for me. Physically, mentally and emotionally.

I'm certain, this book will remind you to slow down… to sit, breathe and live in the present moment and enjoy the little pieces of beauty, life has to offer!

I was sort of enchanted by the beauty of *Serbia* when I got a chance to visit the place a few years ago. Ever since then, I wished to paint its splendour in my own words to push people to visit this place at least once in their lifetime.

Whether you are interested in the rich culture and history of this Eastern European nation or are looking for outdoor adventures, you will see its glory through the eyes of a traveller-a young mother who pushed aside all physical and emotional ties, as well as mother guilt and decided to embark on a journey all for herself. Her experiences are laid out in front of you in the best possible way by adding elements of fiction. All people, especially women, across the world could relate to the emotions spread across the pages. She is opened up to new experiences in life and at the same time bestowed with a feeling of reception to life experiences, tangible and **intangible**.

I fictionalized my own life as a source for my first book, as I believe that's the best way to make it resonate with the readers and get it connected at a deeper emotional level.

Love

Sopna

Dedication

To all those incredible readers who dared to lay their hands on my first book.

Yes, this is for you!!

Contents

Chapter 1 1

Chapter 2 6

Chapter 3 11

Chapter 4 16

Chapter 5 20

Chapter 6 24

Chapter 7 29

Chapter 8 33

Chapter 9 38

Chapter 10 43

Chapter 11 48

Chapter 12 54

Chapter 13 59

Chapter 14 63

Chapter 15 69

Chapter 16 73

Chapter 17 79

Chapter 18 84

Chapter 19	88
Chapter 20	92
Chapter 21	96
Chapter 22	102
Chapter 23	104
Chapter 24	108
Chapter 25	113
Chapter 26	117
About The Author	122

Chapter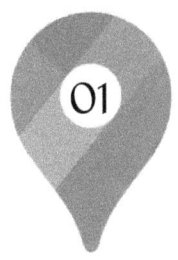

> *"I'm here in this fleeting moment, nowhere else. Just here."*

TIME IS SAID to be fast-paced, but I beg to differ. How can we find something fast-paced when it's been a constant flow ever since time-reading was discovered? It's always in the head; I've never been outside of it. I ponder on these thoughts as I make my way past immigration and to my gate. I don't have time to stop at the duty-free to pick up a neck pillow. *I knew this would happen and I still let it!*

I reach my gate to realize that the flight has been delayed by an hour now. Great, all that rush for nothing, I think to myself as I take a deep sigh.

I dump my bags and situate myself in a cosy nook of the seating arrangement near the gate. I think of picking up the book I left off midway through, maybe two years ago. As I flipped through it, trying to figure out just where I left off, I couldn't help but wonder just why I stopped reading in the first place.

I stop perusing and instead fixate my attention on the people at the airport. People from all walks of life under this one roof, people going to see their loved ones, people going away from their loved ones.

I am snapped out of my thoughts as I hear the call for boarding. I collect my belongings as I make my way to leave this city and its bearings for the next few days. I took my seat, 8A on my flight to *Serbia* and I don't think I left it once. I watched the crew on the runway, sprawled across doing tasks of their own. We're asked to fasten our seatbelts as we prepare for takeoff. I just wonder to myself as I see the land beneath me.

I began planning my *Serbia* trip two months in advance. A thorough research on the place, the people and the type of weather was necessary to expect things I need to be wary of and then you know the usual flights, hotels. Reviews had me exasperated, come to think of it the world literally runs on reviews. Imagine if *Christopher Columbus* had taken down a review from *TripAdvisor* before he set foot in *America*!

Stepping outside the gates of *Nicola Tesla* airport, I look up and down, scanning various name cards, carried individually by men and women, expecting to receive one or another person.

They're all there to serve the same mundane task of receiving someone from the airport, but just different names and different lives, all connected by the same service, to be received.

I spot my name on a blue piece of paper, held high in the air. I don't understand just why my name would even be chosen to be put on a piece of paper that way either. So difficult to read and spot. Odd fellow he must be, I mutter to myself as I make my way to him.

"*Dejan*! Miss! Ah welcome to *Serbia*!" he excitedly greets me. He seems disheveled, almost as if he's been waiting in the same position since last night. I ask him what his name is, he replies, "*Dejan*! Miss!"

Oh. That's what he meant. In fact, I thought it was a *Serbian* greeting.

We quickly exchanged pleasantries and he helped me up with my bags as he escorted me out of the arrival gates. The cold air breezing through the iridescent rays of sunlight engulfs me in a state of acceptance. Poetic some would say, realistic the other.

I'm here. In this fleeting moment, I am here. Here and nowhere else.

Being here in this foreign land all by myself seems like a dream come true for me.

I have almost never had time for myself. I grew up in a home filled with warmth, love and laughter, but I was never left by myself. I believe in seeking solace in the wee hours of the night. Just when everyone's alone with their thoughts. You can hear yourself, just like how you can hear the second's hand dial moving on a clock. You're only able to hear it after you halt. Time doesn't stand still, but you do. Everything else around you do.

This felt like that. I'm in *Belgrade* by myself and for myself. Traveling alone in a city is something I do back in my country of residence, only back home and to work.

And I have travelled a lot alone, for my work and my studies, but not to halt. Not to step back. Not to relax by myself.

But now I'm in a city with no home to return to and no office to go to.

The car *Dejan* drives isn't too shabby, it's his driving skills that are. He doesn't stop for any speed bumps or cracks and crevices on the roads. I almost go shooting through the roof as he passes over a ditch on the road. I snap out of the deep reverie that I was in, taking the scenic route to the mansion that I've booked for myself for my stay. I fall into another rhythmic trance just thinking of the time I am to spend with myself over the coming days.

A well-deserved break from the hustle and bustle of the city. Away from my demanding schedule. Away from the cloudy thoughts that dampen my mood. I sit back, as I breathe and take in every strum from *Chet Baker* playing on my earphones.

A few more bumps along the way and we gush past this street road, to enter the most beautiful view of nature, I have ever seen. The sky was painted with several hues of blue, ethereal rays of sunlight hitting every graze of the earth. I think to myself, just how I wish I could capture this moment in time and live in it forever. My little form of escapism.

Driving swiftly past the swishing grass, we soon arrive at the mansion. What a spectacular scene! I can't believe I'm here.

I don't quite think I've seen a structure as marvellous as this. I rush out of the car to take in the sight of me living here for the days to come. It is situated on a bed of wild grass, out on a lovely patch of land that extends to a huge field, tall standings of oak trees and beech nestle themselves around this mansion. I am instantly consumed by the nature that captivates the essence of this grand house.

Dejan takes my luggage out of the trunk and resists any offers of help from me. I walk through the carefully carved-out cobblestone on the ground and make my way to the grand door that is the entrance of the house.

I notice the way the vines fixate themselves on those pretty French windows as I step closer to the house. Bougainvillea, English Ivy and Elder are the ones I'm able to recognize.

I rap the door in expectation of the host. Thinking it to be an elder lady, just an assumption made on the way the grounds were kept. And boy was I right!

The door opens and greets me with the most arrestingly beautiful woman I've ever seen. Long grey hair, brushed gently to the side. A long white dress with periwinkle floral embellishments hugs her slender frame in the best way. Her skin is bewitching, I believe her to be in her fifties or sixties, she has aged beautifully. I think to myself.

Chapter

> *"Life has its funny ways of reminding us of the little things that truly matter."*

"HELLO AND WELCOME darling, I am *Seira*." she exclaims with such grace. I put my hand out to greet her as she gently pulled me in for a hug. I accept it and almost instantly feel a connection. One of those hugs that just speak to your soul in the best way possible. I feel like I'm home.

"How lovely to meet you, I hope your journey here was safe and relaxing?" She questions.

"It most certainly was, thanks for asking. Your home is beautiful, I don't quite think I've come across a piece of property as marvellous as this." I answer.

She welcomes me with an alluring smile into the house. A grand foyer greets me. It is a special kind of beautiful place; the style was heavily inspired by the Roaring Twenties. As if the house was partly used as inspiration by *F. Scott Fitzgerald* to describe *Jay Gatsby's* mansion. The house retains its original charm by combining contemporary furnishings with a few elements of South Indian heritage and Baroque style decor elements. I felt like I belonged here.

Growing up, I was introduced to a lot of Indian contemporary and Renaissance art. My parents were admirers of art. Art ran through my blood. I felt the special and authentic atmosphere with every step I took in the house. The house was made up of 7 rooms in total.

A grand salon, 3 bedrooms, 2 washrooms, a pantry and a kitchen. As I make my way through the house, I notice tiny glass birds placed on odd counters. Two birds perched on the grandfather clock, almost 7 placed on a vintage piano and three on a window sill.

"Do you play?" I question.

"Yes, I do," she says while putting on a kettle for tea. "Chamomile or Jasmine?"

"Jasmine please," I reply.

"I love the house. Do you permanently live here?" My curiosity deepens.

"I don't, actually. This belonged to my family, starting in the 1800s. My great and how many more greats can I possibly fit into this sentence…" she chuckles, "Grandfather built this for his wife. The house was created to be a welcoming ground for every traveller passing by. I conceptualized his vision and turned it into a vacation rental home, keeping his vision alive."

"How lovely!" I announce.

"There's something I wanted to discuss with you," she says as the kettle shoots steam out.

"I have unfortunately been through a series of unfortunate events which has led me to be stuck out of my home. The pipe broke and my entire house has flooded, I have nowhere else to stay and wanted to check with you if I could possibly stay here for the next two days?"

I think to myself and wonder just how odd this situation is. Does she want to stay here? While renting it out to me? I don't understand and ask her just how she chooses to stay here.

"I would book myself a room at a hotel, but unfortunately, because of the peak tourist season, there aren't any bookings available at decent hotels. "If I'm overstepping my bounds, please let me know." I don't want to cause any hindrances during your stay here at my home."

Though I feel quite irritated, I think about it for a fleeting moment, how could this go wrong? She is the owner of the property anyway. So much safer than being in a situation with anyone else. Plus, it would be good to have a local who can guide me around town and have some level of authenticity to it.

And it's just two days.

"Yeah, of course," I reply with a smile on my face.

"How lovely! Thank you for being so kind. I have shaved off the rental for 2 days because of these unforeseen circumstances and I also want to repay your kindness and understanding." She says.

"There won't be a need for that, I understand it must be difficult, not being at home and being placed with a stranger. I have first-hand experience!" I laugh as I sarcastically reply.

"Oh and she's got a wonderful sense of humour as well! Thank you, darling. You remind me of my daughter."

"Your daughter? Where is she?"

"She's not in town. I haven't seen her in a long time, 15 years to be exact."

"Oh, how come? If I may ask?"

"Just situational, I miss her."

I notice the hesitation and don't probe further. There must be an issue that's probably unresolved, so I leave it at that.

"Honey or sugar?" She asks as she brings the cup of tea to where I'm seated. A wooden high chair at the corner of the kitchen island.

"Honey, please and thank you." I sip from my steaming cup of tea; it burns but I gulp it down. I sting my tongue and accept it.

She walks toward the French window that overlooks the field. The sun is shining and the wind is chilly. She looks out the window, into the air, in hopes of something. I can't figure out just what she's looking at, but there is a sense of longing in her eyes. As I look at her looking into the oblivion, I can't help but wonder whom she reminds me of. I know I've met someone like this in my life, but I can't seem to put my finger on it.

I quietly sip my tea as I notice the glass birds sprawled across the kitchen as well. On the exhaust sill. Two right in the middle of the kitchen island. There are nine on the window sill. 5 on the top sill and 4 on the bottom. I think to myself, what an obsession with birds. I'm sure there's definitely a story behind this.

She seems to be in deep thought, so I quickly shuffle in my seat and get off the stool. I walk down to the main foyer. She soon follows and apologizes for zoning out. I tell her it's alright, I want to explore the property anyway.

"Let me give you a tour!" she announces.

Chapter

> *"Engulfed entirely by nothing but the present moment I'm in."*

I'M LED UP the staircase, which divides into two splits- one leading to the first and second bedroom and the other to the master. The banister is beautiful, dark wood with carvings of floral detailing on it. Original detailing, I think to myself.

She walks like the breeze, ever so nonchalantly. I think to myself, I want to be as graceful as she is when the time comes.

I'm led to the first bedroom, a magnificent nook. A queen-sized bed, with a vague lavender like floral pattern running through the sides and a duvet to match it. The room has an open and fresh layout, with ceiling engravings to resemble a forest, paired with crisp white curtains.

"I'll take this room. I have the master done up for you," she says.

"I don't mind. I'm good with whatever."

"You're a darling," she says gently.

"Come, let me take you to yours," she moves past me as she says.

We walk down a hallway, tiny lamps dawned on a long table leading us to the main room. Right above them are too many frames. Some contained pictures, the others were paintings. I notice the *Greek Landscape's* modern illustration by *Padamsee* or so I think. I ask, "Is this painting by *Akbar Padamsee*?"

"Yes! You've got an eye for art! Do you enjoy academic art?" She gushes excitedly.

"I love post-impressionism and fauvism. I grew up around the art of that style. I was exposed to a lot of *Henri Matisse, Amrita Sher-Gil, Monet, Jamini Roy* and the rest you know."

"I painted that one you see right here. My available time usually involves me painting or reading about painting."

I smile as she says that. My mother loved painting.

This room is unlike any I have been in before. It has a special aura around it. It's engulfing me in a submersed spell. The walls are painted a light hue of brown, more resembling a beige. A French couch just below the window sill, makes a perfect reading corner or just a place to watch the fields or birds.

Birds! Copious amounts of birds surround this room as well.

A few on the curtains and I notice the rod has two birds perched on the corner. A small bird pattern on the nightstand's drawers is engraved. A few tiny birds on the vanity, just daintily lying there.

My eyes light up with a sense of warmth and it reflects. I know because I'm questioned about my satisfaction by her. "I hope these appeal to you?" she asks persuasively. "I like using light colours for the rooms; it opens up the space to great lengths."

"I agree! I do the same. I do appreciate dark colours, but I seem to find myself quite drawn to the light. As metaphoric as it sounds." I respond.

She laughs while agreeing, ever so poised. The room is so phantasmal in its way. It's like stepping into the *Palais de Versailles* and I'm *Marie Antoinette*.

"I have a question, may I?" My curiosity gets the best of me.

"Yes, please go on," she responds.

"Just out of sheer wonder, may I ask how come you have so many glass birds perched on various corners around the house? It's quite interesting."

"I was wondering when you'd ask," she smiles. "When I became a mother, I knew I had a meaning to pass to my daughter. I knew I had one goal in life and one goal only, and that was to make my daughter soar to great heights. Whenever we got some free time, she and I would spend a major portion of our time bird-watching. Almost as if it were one of our hobbies."

She sits down by the window frame as she continues, "My daughter would come from school, eat her lunch, do her homework and come sit with me on the porch, watching birds fly by. We built a birdbath, one summer when she was 7. I believe it to be one of the best days I've lived."

I discern a soft reminiscent sigh.

"The birds and I have a connection. They were my only visiting guests after my daughter's departure to the Middle East. I knew I wanted to fill every place I went to or lived with birds. They were my connection with my daughter and I loved them whole heartedly. Gradually, her availability was restricted because of the life she was building for herself and her family. Birds have to leave their nest eventually, but they always return home when the nights get longer and the days fall shorter."

Wow. I think to myself. I just look at her in awe. The symbolism is truly magnificent in its sweet way.

I reply, "It doesn't explain the positioning though. Don't mind me, I'm just curious. You can choose not to answer if I make this too uncomfortable."

"I choose odd places to perch my birds because of how I want them to remind me, no matter where my eyes land, that one day, my little bird will come back home." she says, smiling.

"Anyway, I'll let you get on with your unpacking. You must be exhausted after all your travels. Let me know if I can help you with anything. I have put in a hot towel box in the washroom and have also heated the water for you to prepare for your bath. Open the top left drawer of the vanity in the washroom to find the spa kit. I used my own recipe to fix you a rose salt scrub," she says influentially.

"Call out to me if I can help with anything and thank you darling angel for accommodating me," she adds.

"You're welcome and I could really use the company. It's the first time I've been away from home, leaving my kids and husband behind for this long."

"Well, I'll be making dinner for us, so I'll see you downstairs at 7 pm."

"I'm looking forward to it and thank you."

As she closes the door behind herself, I turn away and soak in the views past my window.

Chapter

> *"My destination is no longer a place of seeing, but a place of being."*

I SOAK OFF my long travels in the bath as I discover a stack of records near the vanity, adjacent to the record player. *Mohammed Rafi, Frank Sinatra, Kishore Kumar, Ella Fitzgerald* and pure gold, *Lata Mangeshkar*! My oh my! What a true delight!

I take my suitcase and open it to discover my bottle of shampoo has exploded and has left my clothes in ruins. What a disastrous way to enter the evening after having such a beautiful day. I open the wardrobe to find a snappish white robe made of cotton terry and pick it up to approach her for some help.

God this feels ridiculously good on my skin, I think to myself.

I make my way downstairs and I'm greeted by a faint smell of roasted rosemary tomato soup, or so I guess.

I have a pep in my step thinking of the rosemary tomato

soup, my staple comfort food. Soul food, I'd say. Anytime I'm high on emotions, whether upsetting or enticing, I always resort to a great bowl of them.

Asha Bhosle? *Asha Bhosle* is in the background too. Just when I thought my shampoo disaster had put a dampener on my mood. I smile as I make my way to the kitchen.

I'm greeted by her as she gushes over my arrival.

"I see you found the robe! Feels amazing, doesn't it?"

"Supremely fabulous, I must say. It almost feels like my skin is getting gently exfoliated by the material as my skin grazes by it with every movement."

"Please tell me this is tomato soup!" I ask.

"Is so! I was hoping you'd appreciate it."

This is the ultimate comfort food!" I exclaim before she finishes her sentence.

We both laugh together as she swirls the spatula around the cast iron pan.

"Chianti or Pinot Noir?"

"Oh wow, I could definitely go with a glass of Pinot Noir," I respond.

"Hand me those glasses below the sink, would you?"

"Most certainly," I reply. "Which one am I looking at?"

"There's an array of glasses on display. Stem-less, Wide rimmed, Flutes and whatnot."

"Pick out the stem-less, please angel," she requests.

"I have to ask, are you to dine in this robe?" she laughs as she asks.

"Oh my! I completely forgot. I've had a mishap with my luggage. I picked out the worst bottle to store my shampoo in and it seems to have exploded and sent my clothes in ruins. May I please get something to wear for tonight and perhaps tomorrow? Just until I manage to get my clothes washed and dried?"

"Of course, darling. Come along to my room and we'll pick something out for you. And don't worry about your clothes, *Anna*, the housekeeper will be coming in first thing tomorrow. She'll take care of it."

"Oh no, don't worry about that, I can wash my clothes, just please direct me to the washing machine and I'll sort it out."

"Don't be silly! *Anna* comes to the house to take responsibility for its well-being, along with the well-being of its residents. She will take care of it."

"Oh, thank you! I appreciate it."

"Now, come along with me, let's pick out a dress for you," she says as she makes her way to the room.

I notice that she has also changed out of her dress from earlier this morning. She's wearing a deep blue chiffon-like dress, from what I can tell from afar. It's high-necked with long puffy sleeves that cinch in on her wrist. The flow of the dress is so lovely, it's like paint and it flows just where it's directed to. A long, flowy dress that cinches at the waist in the most elegant manner.

Her hair is neatly done in a low bun and is complemented with a pair of these lovely multi-coloured drop earrings.

I think to myself just how fabulous her wardrobe must be, if she pairs this blue dress to go with a simple dinner, I expect nothing less than a *Diane Von Furstenberg* for a quick cup of coffee.

We enter and she asks me to be seated on the vanity stool. The door to her wardrobe is flung open and greets me with the most magnificent view of an array of clothes. I notice that different hues of white and blue seem to stand out from the crowd of the rest. My favourite colours.

"This one!" she exclaims.

A gorgeous white dress stuns me. A midi dress with a gorgeous shine which adds beauty to its silky material awaits me. It has a touch of vintage to it. I can tell by the way it flows.

I take it on and just let it run past my fingers. God, what a dress!

"Earrings!" She walks over to the vanity and opens a chest full of pearls. Earrings, necklaces, rings, bracelets, pearls galore!

A lovely pair of pearl drop earrings are given to me upon insisting that they go well with the dress. I humbly accept, thank her and make my way to my room. "See you downstairs, love."

I smile and nod as I shut the door on my way in.

Chapter

> *"Living life to its entire capacity, tiny moments with yourself are what truly set you free."*

I CAN'T BELIEVE just who looks back at me in the mirror. This can't be me. It's almost as if the dress has given me a whole new persona to my appearance. I take a claw clip and pull my hair back, pulling out two strands from the front to give a cool casual look to it.

Red. I'll need red lipstick to go with this look.

I quickly dab it on and make my way to the kitchen.

"Oh, angel, you look divine," she says.

I smile gratefully. "Your dress has worked its magic on me."

She laughs in disapproval and we make our way to the dinner table.

Chuck Berry plays faintly in the background and various lamps across the room create the best ambiance, harmonized by the candles on the dinner table. I think about how perfect my day has been and how grateful I am for her being around.

Had I been alone and all by myself, I would've spiralled because of the shampoo mishap.

I'm very particular about my things and need them to always go a certain way in my life. I spiral when things are not in my real control. Be it my personal life, my professional life or my social life. I've always been this way. It was inculcated in me ever since I was a little girl. And I have to admit, I hate this nature of mine.

"Come sit?" she asks.

I'm gratified to be here in this fleeting moment. Life has its funny ways of bringing people together.

I gently sit down, worried about the dress, it's like wearing a piece of gold around my body in the form of a dress.

"Wine?" She says and pours it down the glass.

I accept willingly, the start of a great evening, she toasts. To new friends, new journeys and better futures.

"Salud, Salud!" We collectively cheer on.

"Mhmm, this wine is fabulous." I compliment.

"Oh, I'm glad you agree, I'm quite picky when it comes to my wine. I do appreciate a good woody, dry wine. It pairs well with nearly every meal."

She pushes over a plate of stuffed olives and I nearly pounce at it! "Olives are my favourite, especially the stuffed kind," I say excitedly.

"I had a feeling!"

"How so?" I question

"Only because they are the best?"

We laugh in rhythm as we sip down on some more wine.

"I baked some fresh focaccia for us. I hope you enjoy it?" she asks me persuasively.

"Enjoy!? Enjoy would be an understatement. Who doesn't love bread?"

"Absolutely true," she responds in acceptance.

I see the bread being brought out on a platter with its handles replicating branches, with two tiny birds perched on it.

"Smells divine, to say the least!" I announce.

"I'm glad you think so! I am quite obsessed about baking and would always scrounge up the best and most unique forms of bread and cake recipes," she says.

"Bread, wine, olives and oh how can I forget the tomato soup! You are godsent," I tell her. "Thank you, honestly."

"It's so wonderful to have someone around in a new city. A place where you know nobody. A place so foreign to you that making your way back from the field across would come down to be a tedious task."

"I'm glad angel, you've made this old lady's day a whole lot brighter. I don't usually get up to much around the day and today has been nothing but fabulous with you around," she says.

"I'm glad you feel this way. Thank you so much. On my way here, I contemplated if I should've come with my family or friends instead of travelling alone. I knew I wanted to travel alone because it's been on my bucket list for far too long. I needed to do this for myself," I say.

"I work long, excruciating hours that almost never come down to me having any me-time."

I start my days super early, by helping the kids get ready to attend school and dropping them off. Then making my way to the gym for an hour before work. I get dressed at the gym and drive to work, where I'm greeted with an insane supply of work and meetings that never seem to be ending. Getting home from work is my only time alone throughout the day. I head home and my family awaits me for dinner which we religiously have together. The one meal where everyone in the family is present to talk about their individual days and goings."

Of late, I felt a need to do something for myself, hell, I hadn't even gotten a pedicure in over 3 months before I decided to take this trip out.

Chapter

06

> *"Appreciate today for what it is, not for what it can be."*

AS I SAT there, relishing the fleeting moments that kept passing me by in a fanciful state, I knew this moment was something I not only longed for and hoped for, but also one I knew I'd be living soon. The air was rustic, the laughs were merry, the food was fabulous and the company was nothing beyond extraordinary and I was cheered beyond repair. Repair that only required a good amount of shuffling when it came down to it.

I knew that travelling here was going to be the best possible idea for me, especially because of the way that all of this has panned out. The whole idea of being here is finally coming to life now. I can't be any happier than I am in this ephemeral moment.

"You seem to be in a deep reverie of thoughts, some more soup?" she says as I snap out of my thoughts and gladly accept the soup, she holds out for me. "There's a vineyard not too far from here. This time of the year is always the best. Lots of tastings that we can tend to… if you'd like, darling?"

I accept it willingly. I knew I wanted to go test it out myself. The whole idea of it being offered so nonchalantly makes it even better. "Can't wait!" I gleefully respond.

We finish up with dinner. I clear out the dining table as she loads the dishes into the dishwasher.

During a trip, I never enjoy doing daily chores, but this feels different. I don't know or understand how, but it feels super different. I am truly relishing this moment in its fullest capacity. There is never any room for me to complain.

I knew better than to do that. I was raised to be someone who would just take things as they come and always try to make the best use of every situation, no matter what the outcome would've been or could've been. There was always a situation where I knew I had to overcome certain situations in life and this skill made me accelerate them to my best capacity.

"Let's get out to the porch, we can bring the music and situate ourselves on the swing," she announces convincingly.

"Let us, please!" I agree.

We quickly make our way to the swing and place ourselves over there. The air is warm and chilly at the same time. I startle as the air grazes past me, giving me goosebumps.

The moon is lit up in a deep hue of pearl. The light meets the end of the horizon as they carefully blanket each other.

The pearl rays are blind to my eyes, but they leave me perplexed. There is a melancholy hue to the air that I can't see but can feel.

She sits next to me as she fills me up with laughter.

"You know, I can't remember the last time I had a night half as eventfully entertaining as this. Sure, the occasional get-together with my friends and another family, but this feels so different. This is new and different for sure, but this is something I don't think I have experienced in a very long time."

"I have had a difficult few years. My health wasn't doing too well up until recently. Then this whole situation of being alone and not having a family to come home to, it took a toll on me. It was one lonesome evening with myself and my cats when I decided to put up the mansion on a vacation rental home and I don't think I've ever looked back since. There was nothing more that I wanted, but to have a home full of love and laughter. People from all walks of life, from different places across the world, come by and fill my house with love. They fill it with such love that isn't known to this lonesome house either."

"I don't think I have had a connection with anyone this soon in life. There have always been hesitations on my end, every time I pursue a new relationship, regardless of its nature. I grew up rather introverted, but also extroverted at the same time. They label me to be an ambivert. This came out so naturally to me," I tell her. "I was going through a strenuous time and wanted to take a break from my busy schedule, start afresh for a few days in a foreign land with no connections, no ties, just pure living by myself, for myself."

"I was checking through a few websites and I saw your mansion. The constant connection was ridiculously normal and authentic. It felt like I truly belonged. There was nothing but admiration for your piece of land. The photos, by the way, on the website do no justice to it at all. Maybe I could help you out and take some. Better pictures in softer lighting? I want it on the website and on my phone as well. We could dress up tomorrow and get our pictures clicked?" I ask.

"Yes please! I haven't had my picture clicked in so long. I used to model when I was young, though."

"I had a feeling of the sort!" I excitedly gushed. "You have maintained yourself quite marvellously. I need to learn from you!"

"Thank you, darling angel. I guess living here in the countryside seems to have worked its magic on me."

We can hear a faint tune by Chuck Berry playing in the background, as crickets chirp by and the moonlight serenades us individually. She is in her trance and me, in my own, but we're here together.

"Can I ask you something?" she asks.

"Please, anything," I announce.

"How come you decided to visit *Serbia*? Of all the places across the world to choose from, how come you decided to go ahead with this country?"

"Wow! Nobody has asked me that. From planning to my departure, nobody asked me just why I chose *Serbia* to travel to, alone. Thank you for asking me this. I appreciate it."

"I have, we have always been fascinated by the Balkan region and to have to be here at this present time has been a dream of mine. I have always been a history aficionado and knew that I wanted to have this trip pay homage to my first discovery. A place not too far from home as well. Somewhere I could easily get on and get off. I researched endlessly for a good amount of time before I selected just where I was to travel and decided, I would be coming down to *Serbia* for my excursions." I pause, looking out at the wilderness and then continue, "I knew it was a smart decision and look! I'm here with you! I don't think I've connected with anyone as quickly as I have with you."

I hold her hand in mine. "Thank you for being so welcoming. I appreciate it in the highest regard."

Chapter

> *"Life shouldn't be experienced;*
> *It should be lived. Bravely and happily."*

WE SIT IN silence for the next few passing moments, we both know we're grateful to be in each other's presence at this point. My life with my own commitments, she with her own. It almost feels as if, we both are individually seeking solace in each other's company here.

Life has its funny way of introducing you to people whom you would not even fathom to be someone you would hold in high regard. Whether it's someone you pass by on the street or someone you may meet at a café, whomever it may be, you can never know when life turns around and holds on to people who will be around.

We chat for hours on end, about our childhoods, our interests and our hobbies and soon come to find that the sun is now rising. I look across the field in awe. The sky is painted this beautiful deep shade of orange and crimson flashes by in streaks, much like a watercolour brush stroke. The clouds part and make way for the majestic sun that comes up in such a regal manner. Flushing every corner with the tangiest shades of orange, yellow and red.

The birds are up and about, chirping melodiously and fixating themselves on the branches of various trees sprawled across the field. There is a beautiful tune in the air, it's swamping me in the most rhythmic trance.

I have seen various sunrises in my many years of existence. But none like this.

None like this at all!

The moment is passing me by and I'm trying my best to hold onto it, but it's fleeting. It's fleeting and I'm deciding to hold onto it so tight, I don't want to let go.

I am, reminded of my mother as I watch the clouds take shape in the sky.

I can see her profile. I can see her.

She's there, painted magically by the sun's rays and looking beyond ethereal as she does. I am captivated magically by the various hues and my eyes are lit up like flames - because of the reflection of the sky in front of me.

My mother created a wonderful world for me. She never gave me the idea that I couldn't do anything I wanted to do or be whoever I wanted to be. She filled our house with love, fun, art, lessons and music unflagging in her efforts to create the best role model for me. As she guided me through those lovely incredible years of me growing up and developing, I don't think she knew that the person I most wanted to be like was her.

Chapter

*"Life shouldn't be experienced;
It should be lived. Bravely and happily."*

WE SIT IN silence for the next few passing moments, we both know we're grateful to be in each other's presence at this point. My life with my own commitments, she with her own. It almost feels as if, we both are individually seeking solace in each other's company here.

Life has its funny way of introducing you to people whom you would not even fathom to be someone you would hold in high regard. Whether it's someone you pass by on the street or someone you may meet at a café, whomever it may be, you can never know when life turns around and holds on to people who will be around.

We chat for hours on end, about our childhoods, our interests and our hobbies and soon come to find that the sun is now rising. I look across the field in awe. The sky is painted this beautiful deep shade of orange and crimson flashes by in streaks, much like a watercolour brush stroke. The clouds part and make way for the majestic sun that comes up in such a regal manner. Flushing every corner with the tangiest shades of orange, yellow and red.

The birds are up and about, chirping melodiously and fixating themselves on the branches of various trees sprawled across the field. There is a beautiful tune in the air, it's swamping me in the most rhythmic trance.

I have seen various sunrises in my many years of existence. But none like this.

None like this at all!

The moment is passing me by and I'm trying my best to hold onto it, but it's fleeting. It's fleeting and I'm deciding to hold onto it so tight, I don't want to let go.

I am, reminded of my mother as I watch the clouds take shape in the sky.

I can see her profile. I can see her.

She's there, painted magically by the sun's rays and looking beyond ethereal as she does. I am captivated magically by the various hues and my eyes are lit up like flames - because of the reflection of the sky in front of me.

My mother created a wonderful world for me. She never gave me the idea that I couldn't do anything I wanted to do or be whoever I wanted to be. She filled our house with love, fun, art, lessons and music unflagging in her efforts to create the best role model for me. As she guided me through those lovely incredible years of me growing up and developing, I don't think she knew that the person I most wanted to be like was her.

I want to look away from the blazing sky, but I can't. I am quite literally trapped by the appearance of my mother in the sky. It's been long since I last saw her. I think to myself.

I'm snapped out of my trance by her call.

"Sweetie, let's get to bed. We've been up all night. We'll sleep and wake up by noon to get started with our day - I have to show you around!"

I agree as we make our way back into the grand foyer.

I feel dazed as we walk upstairs, making our way to our respective rooms of slumber. My hands graze past the banister and I feel electrified, the house has so much history. I smile to myself as I wonder just how many choices, I have made in my life that have led me to this very moment.

There is a great deal of positive energy in this house. Much like butterflies doing the waltz over a hot summer day, passing by the cool breeze over a strawberry field.

We make our way upstairs and end our soiree with a hug, I feel warmth at this moment as I hug her.

Her hug feels like eating a cinnamon roll on a cold, snowy day by the fireplace. One of those hugs that captivates you - your Mind, Body and Soul.

One that leaves you grateful for every moment.

We bid our goodbyes and leave to enter our rooms.

I walk into my room and take the night's events off me. I have had a wondrous first night in this foreign land. I can't help but smile because of how happy I am at this moment.

I undo the duvet and slip into bed, letting my muscles relax, letting myself relax.

Chapter 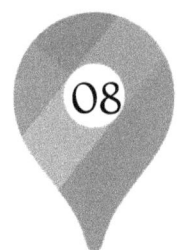 08

> *"One moment here, one moment there.
> Time is our teller, our teller of all."*

I AM WOKEN up by a faint smell of coffee.

Feeling suspiciously well-rested and not dazed at all, I attribute it to how wonderfully well I felt the whole night. It's odd because a whole day of travelling and a whole night of staying up rarely seem to do the trick.

The cool air breezes through the glass panes as the crisp white curtains flow rhythmically along with the breeze.

It looks enchanting. The French windows with the sun's rays hitting it so magically. I find myself moving towards the washroom to freshen up.

I quickly took a cold shower and got dressed. God, I feel so good and refreshed after the shower.

I pick out a white linen dress to go for the day. It's long and breezy, perfect for a stroll down *Belgrade*. I rummage through my bag to find my espadrilles and straw hat to match. Happy that at least some of my belongings were saved from the shampoo mishap.

I find an interesting bottle of perfume on the vanity. The make appears vintage, with the pump and all attached.

A beautiful crystal bottle with a baby pink pump. I pick it up and spray the tiniest bit to catch a whiff of it.

It smells like a pretty spring season. I can't quite describe it as anything else but that.

Notes of Orange, Cardamom, Roses… and whatnot.

The smell feels wistful, a place like home. A wave of pure nostalgia just blankets me.

I drowse myself in it as I make my way towards that heavenly smell of coffee being roasted.

Morning sunshine!" she says delightfully. "Did you sleep well?"

"Morning morning! Oh, fabulously well thank you, how did you sleep? I assume well enough because of this cheery start!" I respond.

"Thank you! Coffee? I've just roasted a fresh batch. It tastes even better than it smells!"

"Don't mind if I do!"

She pours me a cup of coffee in a beautiful hand-painted yellow mug, it feels so nice to hold a warm cup of coffee on a beautiful sunny but chilly day.

The coffee is nothing but a true delight as I take in a sip. I feel electrified, to say the least. It's the perfect roast with the faintest caffeine and tobacco note. Just perfect. **Black coffee, as intense as me.** I chuckle and think to myself.

"All right so! Let me tell you what I have planned for the day!" she gushes excitedly.

"Do tell do tell!" I respond in equal excitement.

"So! We're starting with *Old Belgrade*! We'll be off to the *National Museum*, followed by a horseback riding session!" she announces. "From there, we'll head down *Knez Mihailova Street*. You know, this street is named after *Mihailo Obrenović III, Prince of Serbia*. It is one of the beautiful streets to stroll on in an evening with many mansions across built during the late 1870s.

And make some budget to get some shopping done! You must have a look at the locally handcrafted teapots and tiny trinkets! I am sure you will love the place."

"This all sounds exciting, but please tell me where food fits in?" I ask quite mischievously.

"Food would never go amiss! The amalgamation of the eastern and western cultures brings a uniqueness to the *Serbian* dishes, making it an excellent choice for travel-eaters looking to try something new while visiting."

"For a caffeine fix, we'll be turning onto *Kralja Petra Street* to experience some of *Belgrade*'s best coffee from *Cafe&Factory6's* on-site roastery!"

"Wow! This sounds interesting!" I gush over.

"This certainly is, isn't it!"

From going down to having a shifting work schedule - to dealing with a bunch of different moments in my social and personal life. I felt happy about investing in myself, i.e.; my travel.

I never once experienced having a moment of clarity in terms of rolling my day out. I knew I needed to live in this moment and accept it for what it is. I know this is a moment I truly deserve for myself.

We quickly hurried up and I downed my coffee. We grab our things and make our way to the streets of *Belgrade*. I am nothing but happy to hurry up and rush!

I reflect on certain moments in life where I have never been exposed to not rushing. Every single thing has almost always been rushed for me.

Anna, the caretaker is waiting outside the mansion doorway, with the car key. I accept it happily. I walk outside the mansion, onto the driveway and I'm greeted by a blue convertible! Upon inspection, I realize that it is a *vintage 1953 Chevy Corvette.*

I squeal in excitement and jump into the car.

"Wow! I didn't know you appreciated convertibles this much or I would've pulled it out earlier."

"I love them! Though I'm a novice I'm also quite inclined to learn more!" I tell her.

I am really happy to take this beauty for a spin. The sun has us basking under its rays today and the wind has us dancing to her breeze.

Because of how unknown I am to the roads of this glorious city; I request that she be my human GPS tracking system, but she laughs. She laughs because she herself is unbeknownst to the streets of this city. I then pull out my phone in hopes of that piece of technology guiding us to our location.

This feels surreal to the greatest extent. Driving in a city with no clue to directions, but with such beautiful sights to offer. I am living in moments that I never want to end.

Chapter

> *"Happiness isn't found, it is created.*
> *Moments of joy easily reciprocate to*
> *happiness we create for ourselves in the present."*

THERE IS A lot to see and a whole lot more to do. Having to travel across the country with someone I've known for a day is quite insane if you ask me. Maybe my trust issues haven't ever acted up, but this is where I start to deduce and live free as it comes.

Que sera, Sera. Whatever will be, will be.

This is how I intend to continue to live, I think to myself as we zoom past the trees and onto the highway.

The sun is shining bright as we drift past other cars. I'm wearing my straw hat, but I have also secured it with a scarf to not lose it. I remember the memories I have attached to this scarf.

I knew that if I took this woollen scarf that my mom had knitted for me on my worldly excursions, I would slightly put myself at risk of losing it while doing so.

But again, this was a turning point for me as well, because I knew I wanted to start moving differently. Differently does not necessarily have to relate to being something negative or bad, but something that I gladly will accept for whatever it is.

I think the difference might stem from being something that doesn't necessarily have to relate to your ideas, but it also relates to something that you may not intensely visualize but may cause an acceptance of.

I think about moments that have zoomed past me, whatever they may be. When I was younger, when I wasn't as young and me, now older. I smile.

I am once again snapped out of my thoughts by her; she plays the next song on the playlist as we make our way down to the main city.

We both cheerfully sing along as we stride towards town.

Driving past, we slow down because of some oncoming traffic. Only for it to reveal a van that has broken down on the side of the road. As far as I can tell, there's a group of 4 young girls, just on the side of the road, wearing caps and fanning themselves with a newspaper.

I pull up on the side and we get out of the car.

We walk towards them.

We come to learn that they're a group of university-going best friends who are here on a girl's trip!

"*Ella, Noel, Zima* and *Nina*! How lovely to meet you girls. How can I help? Are you girls waiting on recovery for your van here?"

"We are actually!" *Nina* half-whines. "We've been stuck on the side of the road for over an hour now and nobody seems to be coming to our rescue. It is such an inconvenience. We are only in *Belgrade* for another 3 days and we haven't been able to move along with our plans because of this hitch."

The other girls sigh and chime in.

I sympathize with them and suggest hitching a ride with us. "How about you girls come along? We're going down to the main city anyway, might as well catch a ride with me!"

"Yes! If that's not an inconvenience!" exclaims *Ella*.

"Come on in then!" I say.

I knock down the front seat as the girls scramble at the back. Two sit on the seat while the other two sit on each other's laps.

Oh, to be young! I think to myself.

The girls laugh as we blaze through the highway… I catch a glance at her as we ride. She looks back at me and gives me a reassuring smile as I do.

I feel so young and blooming at this moment. I feel free at this moment right now.

We quickly make our way to the main town and park. The girls then ask us to join them for a river kayaking experience!

River kayaking? I think to myself as I wonder just how I am about to refuse this offer. I would be up for anything, be suspended from a high-rise building, go ride a huge rollercoaster, go zip-lining over a mountain. But kayaking, absolutely no.

I have always been super scared of the water. Large beds of water to be specific.

There is a whole world unknown to us and that world is called the world beneath the surface of the ocean. Or river in this case.

Horror movies don't scare me; undiscovered sea creatures do. We have left the planet earth and gone to space to discover life, but what about the ocean? Only 7% of the ocean has been discovered by us. The remaining 93% remain a mystery. We genuinely do not know.

As I pull myself out of these ever-so-consuming thoughts of marine life and the ocean that hasn't been discovered, I reject the idea instantly in my mind. I really do.

I will not be on a piece of plastic, with a flimsy life vest, rowing another piece of plastic to get me places, on top of being placed on waters that I have no control over.

But then again, I am presented with some level of conflict in my mind. What could actually go wrong? It's not like I'd be alone and all by myself, I would have all these girls around me.

I've done things very differently than how I normally would before and it seems to have worked out in my favour over the past few days, so how could something possibly go wrong?

I take a deep breath and agree to their suggestion. "Let's go!" I reply grinning but terrified on the inside.

Chapter

"Slow yourself down, slow things down and just watch how beautiful they become."

WE ZOOM PAST the highway as we now descend down to the river bed that awaits our arrival. The sun is out and there's a beautiful, chilly breeze that hits my face as we stride down to the dock.

As we hop out of the car, I feel my weight getting heavier on my foot with each and every step that we take towards the dock of the rafts. They float so calmly in those tepid waters.

"I'm so excited! This might be the only excitement I might not be able to control on this trip. I've been planning this out for so long!" *Noel* squeals in excitement, as she announces this to the group. She has a pep in her step. The excitement just radiates through her and I can't help but smile because this might just be a positive experience. I don't want my mind to continuously hold me back from such an adventure of my lifetime!

"Are you not excited?" *Nina* asks me, as she notices that I haven't said much in a while.

"Hey, if you don't feel comfortable, please don't put yourself through it. I'll stay back with you if you don't wish to come along on the raft ride," she continues.

Seira is beside me all the time. I notice that she is staying silent with an ever-charming smile on her beautiful lips.

"No. Not at all. I mean, I definitely am a little out of my element, but that has nothing to do with you girls suggesting this activity. I am scared for sure, but I think I just need a push sometimes. Don't you worry about me, I'm in safe hands with you girls!" I reply.

They smile and grin collectively as we all walk on the huge spread of grass toward the kayaks.

The bed of water is extraordinarily beautiful. Its blue is perfectly accessorized by the green grass. This lake could swallow me alive; I think to myself.

We arrive and are greeted by the raft instructors.

"Hello and welcome! I am *Zachary*, your instructor for today. You are a group of such pretty ladies, where are you all from?"

We briefly introduce ourselves and are then taken down to this waiting room-like station that has a huge array of life jackets! I take a deep breath as I take this all in. There are a bunch of people scattered across the room - women, men and children of all ages. All excited, trying on the lifejackets to find a perfect fit!

How are they this excited, to get onto a plastic boat with nothing but deep, dense oblivion below? I really stress out as I think to myself.

As I accept it for what it is, we are taken down to the dock by *Zachary*. He explains the basics of how to handle yourself should the boat tip over and I couldn't help but stress out, thinking, *'What if the boat actually did?'* I am then reassured by his positive affirmations of how that has never happened and that only if a great supreme external force were to do so, would it ever happen. And then again, what supreme external force would that even be? I wouldn't even dare to have such a thought, let alone have a visual force to it.

I have picked out a pink and orange coloured life jacket for myself. My two happy colours. Orange is said to make you feel energized and enthusiastic! Two feelings that I could most definitely use right about now. Whereas pink is said to have a calming effect on people. Two complete opposites of what I should most definitely be using right about now. I really laugh at how silly I can be sometimes.

We hop onto the kayak and they secure us with a belt, I sit at the back while *Seira* sits in front of me, because I'm too scared to place myself at the front. We are collectively given a pair of oars. One for her and one for me.

Noel and *Zima* are right beside us, while *Nina* and *Ella* are still waiting to be seated and allotted a kayak. We jointly wait for the two of them and as we do, I look down, into the water. Scared of seeing something I wouldn't like to see in the water, I quickly brush myself off and look at the sky. What a magnificent day. The sky is a perfect blue, and white cotton candy clouds adorn the sky so perfectly. There is a lot of background noise I'd say, much like background music, but I'm okay with it.

Chatter from the people surrounding us, birds chirping, gentle lake sounds of the water crashing the side of the dock, the gentle swishing of the trees around us, a faint sound of the traffic and lots and lots being contributed by my inner monologue of how happy and terrified I am at the same time.

Nina and *Ella* have them moved along to the boat that arrives on our left; the two people in it are such beautiful ladies. It seems like they're grandmother and granddaughter. The younger girl is in the front and is the first to get up as well. She quickly makes her way to the ledge with the help of one of the instructors. She moves toward her grandmother to help her get out of the kayak. They leave and are chirpy while they walk off the ledge.

My mother and I would spend various Sunday afternoons sitting by the lake or in parks. She would lay out a delicious picnic spread, consisting of freshly squeezed orange juice, fresh bread, homemade cakes and snacks. We would then spread out a picnic mat and sit there by the lake for endless hours just talking about life. She would pass on her wisdom to me, things she learned at my age, her do's and don'ts. The usual.

We would then discuss whatever she was reading that month, I say month because finishing it in a week was very difficult. With a house to run, kids, a husband and herself to manage, reading a book was a very difficult task for her to take up, regardless of how passionate or not she was.

We would then bird watch and observe the flora around us. This is where all of my knowledge of flowers and gardening comes from.

Once again, I am broken out of my trance by *Nina* and *Ella*, as the four girls chime in and start cheering me on, especially since I express just how scared I am about the whole situation, which is rather sweet but I can't help but find myself getting more nervous and feeling singled out.

I feel embarrassed and so I ask them to stop, which they do not resist at all. In fact, I even jokingly say so, but they are supremely respectful. We all give our one last hurrah and the girls start oaring away. I still haven't even held my oars in the right way is what I think to myself, how on earth am I to move it according to the safety protocols and enjoyment levels simultaneously?

Chapter

> *"What is fear anyway? Pre conceived notions or first-hand experiences. You are always greater than your fear."*

I GAIN MOMENTUM and start rowing the boat. *Seira* and I were doing the same, a little flustered, but all were going well.

We soon find ourselves in a rhythm of flow. The wind is blowing well and was zooming past tepid waters. The air and water are gleaming with every paddle through them. The ripple caused by each swift movement of my oar makes this moment very enjoyable in its own sense.

Perhaps there isn't much harm done in this situation.

Perhaps I may have overestimated the intensity of this situation.

Perhaps I shouldn't have been this scared to have even tried considering this experience in any way, shape or form.

I don't think I have ever been this delighted to be in the water.

I would shy away from entering the water when I was younger, only because I had a horrendous swimming instructor who would give me the toughest time even dabbling in the water.

He reminds me of a supremely strict individual, may be because of his rigid built or tonality of his voice or his strict intense regime that he puts little children under. I don't know what it was, but I do remember him chucking me in the pool this one time I refused to enter it. Yes, it was bad. Just as bad as reading this is.

I don't understand just how at ease I am now.

From being super scared of dipping my feet, even at the shallow end of a pool to being so comfortable with sitting on a piece of board rowing away to glory on a majestic river. This experience has been nothing short of a dream for me. I have nothing negative to get exposed to from this entire experience.

The whole journey has been super surreal for me.

We row our boat to the centre of the river as we all come by and just park ourselves near each other.

The sun is now setting and the way it meets the *Danube river* is nothing short of a painting by *Claude Monet*. The whole lay of the nature is picturesque.

Nobody breaks the silence. We just sit there in peace and awe of this whole experience. I have never once been this mesmerized by the water.

The water is so feminine. It gleams as the orange rays of the sun paint it with a deep tinge of the sky.

Everything standing still for me at this very moment. Nothing can break me out of it at all. *Noel*, *Nina*, *Zima*, *Ella* and *Seira* are just sitting with me. We're all in our thoughts and nobody dares to break this silence. We're not seeking solace within it, but I know we've all now found our tiny flying moment of escapism. Regardless of how short-lived it may feel at this point. I know we have a lot to say, but nothing to say.

The silence is interrupted by a tiny bird that comes by and perches itself on my boat. I can't help but wonder whether this is a sign from the universe, to let myself fly and just not look back. The bird stays in the sky all day, flying from one place to another, how peculiar of it is to come by the water and just land on my very boat that too. It must have felt drawn to our energy, I'm certain. That's how birds are anyway, they're the first to sense energy of any kind, positive or negative.

We, women come from different walks of life, are of different age groups and have different places of residence as well and here we are, kayaking in the *Danube River*, with the moon waking up from its deep slumber, with the sparkling rays of sunlight and cheerful laughter as the water ripples by, creating the most charming sound. It feels like my soul has been nourished. My soul, which has been starved of nature of late. I can feel it now.

It's kind of like, you don't realize what you've lost until it goes away. I feel like that, in this present moment.

We should never let one bad experience make us resent a certain thing. Whether tangible or intangible, there shouldn't be a hold back from situations. Accepting them for what they are, is what makes us human.

I wouldn't know just how I would accept the open waters until I spent some time on them, in a calm, relaxed state.

This happens exactly when our mind, body and soul accept it for what it is. I ask myself just why. I reason it out to be a situation where acceptance has the biggest role to play. Only majorly because we are now receptive to how we truly feel in this fleeting moment. Reality has figured out just where the negatives and positives truly lie.

Seira asks me how I feel, "You okay now? All good?"

"Quite frankly, I don't think I've ever felt better."

"I could tell, you look like you've gone into a mode of acceptance. I can't say why, but there's a look in your eyes. I feel deeply reminded of my younger self. I had the utmost control over various things but somehow, I found that control slipping away, I knew I had to do something, but at the same time, I somehow enjoyed it slipping away. It sounds rather odd, but that's life's funny way of showing you to just live in the present moment. As you are now," she says softly.

"I think I may have been too much of an overthinker, not in this regard, but in a generalized sense. I mean, who doesn't enjoy holding power or control, but to be fair, it is so nice to just let go sometimes," I reply.

She looks at me intently and just smiles. Her eyes look so soft. Like I've been embraced into a hug. Like she knows, I could do with one. She simply puts her hand out to me. As I hold it, I feel nothing but a true sense of belonging. Some people just hold such power. Kind of like, I'm here and the rest has just faded away entirely.

We take turns shifting between places on the boat, *Seira* and I in the centre first, then *Nina* and *Ella* and so on. We talk about our journeys here, the way our lives have shifted since coming here and everything that plays a part in our lives, while we make our way back to the dock. Before we leave our spot in the lake, I look down at the water.

I am no longer afraid to see whatever may greet my eyes. I'm ready to accept it. I am no longer afraid at all. I look below to find the most exquisite view to greet my eyes. There's not too much marine life here, but I notice enough to help me appreciate what I thought I wasn't ever going to.

Maybe the use of the word 'appreciate' isn't too well received but that is nothing but the truth that I deem. I know for a fact that although this was the first time I have been greeted by marine life, it certainly won't be the last.

This trip has made me very receptive. I am open to acceptance, towards many things as it is.

We then swiftly row ourselves back to the dock and find the other girls, who greet us at the foot of the ledge. They helped us out of the kayak as we return the borrowings to the instructor. As we make our way back to the car and away from the river, I stop, pause and look back at this grand view. This grand late afternoon that I have had for myself. They all call out to me as they notice me standing by myself and I request them to situate in the car, announcing that I'd be back in a bit.

I walk towards the water and find a small spot of land that extends outwardly to the river. It is small enough to fit a single person. Like it was made for me!

I stand there and take it all in. I do this because I know I will never experience this feeling again. Yes, similar to it for sure, but never the same exact feeling.

I know that, nothing in life can ever be replicated, duplicated yes, but never replicated. A single line here, a single line there, never the same.

Chapter

> *"No expectations and no disappointment, there is just acceptance."*

AS I STAND there by the river, I notice a small family of ducks. They swim in this one peaceful corner, a corner where the water greets the land very peacefully. The mother is swimming to and fro as if she was searching for something. I then notice a baby duckling a little far away from her. I deduce she's looking for her little one. I quickly get off that piece of land and make my way to the baby duckling. I take off my espadrilles and march onto the duckling. It looks frightened to see me walk towards it; I gather and shift my stride to a more welcoming one as opposed to the hurried one. It understands and stays put in its position. I cup it gently and bring it back to where the mother kept prancing to and fro. It is now reunited with its other duckling brothers and sisters. The mother looks relieved as she rushes back to it and swims near the family.

I can't help but let out a gentle laugh. How beautiful! Even in nature, our motherly instincts never stop. Something as tiny as a duck knew that her baby was missing and she did everything in her power to search for it.

I notice a bench and sit there for a few more moments, just a few. Just until the sun says goodbye.

I will miss this place. I know I truly will. I've taken many trips before, but none like this. Maybe because I've always taken them with my family or friends and this was my first solo. But something just seems so different about this place. I feel so welcomed in this land.

It has greeted me with open arms and fully embraced me for who I am. Not who I can be, not who I was, not who I will possibly be in the future. There are no ties to this place, no expectations and no disappointment, there is just acceptance. One of the most beautiful things in life is acceptance. Taking it for what comes.

Many shy away from acceptance. Mainly because we've been conditioned to believe that the first offer is never good enough, regardless of its nature. Why counter it, is what I find myself asking. Life is simple, we just complicate it.

Us humans, freaks of nature that we are, are bound by an insatiability of wants. Having to accept is a manner of the highest regard, because there weren't any expectations, to begin with.

Well, maybe there were, but nobody is ever truly satisfied down to a T. We are programmed to feel differently, whether it is 0.01% or 100%.

As I find myself in this deep trance of thoughts, I acknowledge that my time spend here will be exploited in the best possible manner. Mainly because I owe it to myself and the people around me.

I hear someone calling out to me and as I look behind, I find all the girls coming back. They're all hand in hand, smiling as they notice me by myself.

"May we please join?" *Zima* questions me in hope.

"Please! Make yourself at home." I respond, as I slowly nudge myself to the corner of the bench to make some space for the girls.

Nina and *Noel* positioned themselves on the grass below, while *Ella*, *Zima* and *Seira* positioned themselves on the bench, sitting next to me.

For the next 15 minutes or so, nobody says a word. We just watch the beautiful sun go down to retire for the day. We listen to the tiny waves of the water hit the small bed of rocks by the shore, the duck family prance around and about, the chatter of people at the docks, the swishing of the trees, the lullabies being sung to the baby birds in their nests. Everything feels like it belongs.

We then get up and prepare ourselves to head back to the car. Nobody really says much, mainly because we just had a tête-à-tête with ourselves. We said what we had to say. Nothing more, nothing less.

The sun has now gone down and there's now nothing warm to wrap around us. The air is now briskly chilly. We bring up the roof of the car as we make our way back into the city.

"Let us get dinner at this quaint little restaurant I know of. They serve the freshest, warmest bread, with such perfect food to go along with." *Ella* announces.

"Yeah!!!" We cheer in unison as we announce that we're all equally starved.

We drive down to the opposite side of the river and we are greeted by the most perfect view of this restaurant that's situated by the waterfront.

The restaurant looks inviting. It is dawned with tiny lights, a brick structure just perfectly matching it in the best possible way. The entrance is carved magically - A French rustic door with brass panelling on the side. The whole ambiance is just perfect.

We make our way inside as we are greeted by the faint smell of bread and a lovely symphony of saxophones. I suspect it to be *Charlie Parker*. I am truly riveted to be here, with such great company, great music, great food and heavenly views.

The host greets us and welcomes us to a table at the corner. The table is just perfect. It is situated by the corner of the ledge, overlooking the river in the moonlight. The *Danube* has truly shined her inner goddess in the most noir way. There's a live quartet playing not too far from us as I scan the room for this phantastic sound of music.

I sit down next to *Seria* at the round table we're at. We're all starving to the core as the waiter arrives at our table and we nearly pounce on him for the menu. I scan through it and realize I shall be having nothing but a good, comforting plate of pasta. Black truffle fettucine for me and only me.

Everyone places their orders and we're presented with a huge basket of warm, freshly baked bread. Bread of varied sorts and butter with pesto. Just when I thought my day couldn't get any better than it already was.

I close my eyes and just ask for blessings at this moment. I have built a lovely family in a land so foreign to me, I wouldn't even know how to pronounce the next street's name.

"I'm very glad to be here, ladies. I must say, I don't think I've truly been at such ease in a very long time. I feel like I have not just one, but 5 daughters. Thank you all for being you. I am truly riveted to be in each of your companies today. Thank you." *Seira* says in the most gratified manner.

I raise my glass and say "Touché," but just as I do so, all the girls shoot me the most peculiar glance.

I question them, "What happened, did I pronounce it wrong?" because the word being French and because of French being my weakness.

"No, nothing, I don't know why we did that. We thought we heard something in the distance behind you." *Noel* says as she speaks on behalf of the other girls.

Chapter

"There may be more captivating experiences in life, but this one is ours."

I LOOK BACK to see if there actually is something, but my eyes are greeted by the beautiful moon shining on the river. Nothing else at all.

The discussion is then quickly shifted as we are presented with our plates of food.

I am a complete child! I think to myself. I don't even wait a second until the plate lands in front of me before I stuff my face with the plate of goodness.

This is heaven. This truly is heaven. Heaven on earth is a French restaurant that has a live music playing *Charlie Parker*, by the lakeside, especially when you are starving for the whole day!

We wrap up dinner not too late after the first bite and we order for dessert. The night ends with a nightcap each and we make our way to the car.

We say our goodbyes to the girls, as they live not too far from the restaurant and we exchange numbers.

Such lovely girls, I think to myself.

Seira and I get into the car as we head back to the mansion after such a tiring day. All I can think of right now is washing off my long day in a hot shower and slipping into a pair of my silk pyjamas, right into the duvet. A nice faint tune by *Stan Getz* plays in the background as I sip into a hot cup of chamomile tea. Ah bliss.

"Thank you for today." I tell her as I ride to the main gates of the mansion.

"Thank you? What for?" she questions.

"I don't think I've had a day as wondrous as today was, in a very long time. So so long ago that I can't even remember. I don't think I'll have the heart to say goodbye to you, to this place, to these memories, to this beautiful home, when the time comes. Until then, I won't say a word about my departure and neither will I think of it. I will be doing nothing but living in the moment. Without a single care in the world," I announce.

"Way to go! You're not like how I remember you to be when we first met!" she says, "You've changed. You seem different."

"Different?" I question.

"Yes, something is different about you. I can't define it, but something is certainly different. It's a good difference, please don't take it the wrong way," she goes on.

"Yes, I feel different. I completely agree with you," I say.

She smiles back in reassurance as I drive into the garage of the mansion. We exit and make our way to the grand foyer and we are greeted by *Anna*, the housekeeper.

"Hey, *Anna!* How are you?" I ask her.

"Very well ma'am thank you. I hope you've had a lovely day! Your clothes have been washed and ironed. I have placed them in your wardrobe," she responds.

"Perfect! thank you so much, I really appreciate it," I speak.

We say our goodbyes to Anna as she leaves for the night, and we make our way to the kitchen.

"Hot Chocolate?" she offers.

"Don't mind if I do!" I chuckle.

I love hot chocolate! Ending the entire day with a cup of cocoa seems about right. The whole day was perfect and this was to be the cherry on top of the cake. She put down a pot of milk and got out a bag of cacao powder. I helped arrange the cups and pulled out a surprise bag of tiny marshmallows.

I sat down on the kitchen island and looked at the glass birds again. Ah, those birds, my other friends in this house.

"You're observing the birds, aren't you?" she asks.

"Yes, I remember you telling me why you placed them all across the house. You know, it makes a lot of sense now. The whole arrangement of having the birds scattered across the house. You like being reminded of your daughter, don't you?" I ask.

"I do, yes. I miss her dearly, but there's nothing that I can do about it now. She's living her life elsewhere and I don't blame her. She had a lovely childhood and an even better upbringing. I knew for a fact that when she left, she would like to explore other places. She has always been a free spirit. A spirit that likes constant change and shift, but at the same time, she also really appreciates coming back home. She knows that at the end of the day, regardless of how fast-paced your life may be, you have to come back home," she went on to say.

I was thinking of how healthy would have been the relation she and her daughter had. I can undoubtedly say that the daughter was raised in a very wholesome environment where her mother not only listened to her needs but took them into consideration as well.

Communication is one thing, comprehension is another. I can imagine that at the end of the day, regardless of what the daughter did, she could always go up to her parents and have a healthy conversation with them about it.

Having a healthy relationship with people you love and care for, always reciprocates to building a greater connection with them in the long run.

Chapter

*"The world changes by the view it is perceived by.
Change it. You have the power to."*

THE POT COMES to a boil as the hot chocolate nearly spills out. She rushes to the stove and I place out the cups for us. She pours it down and I top it off with the tiny marshmallows.

"Darling, open up that top left drawer of the kitchen island, would you?" she requests.

"Yes, of course! What do I bring out?"

"The shortbread please, they go so well with the hot chocolate!"

The way everything has worked out for me in such a perfect manner today just makes me want to pinch myself! Maybe I'm living in a dream. This just feels so bizarre to me. I know that, this may sound silly but it is really the little pleasures in life that matter. Always the little pleasures.

They are what truly brings us together.

When I am having a bad day at work, I know my only fix would be a nice sloppy pizza.

If I want to destress, can anything be better than a nice hot bath with my rose salts?

To celebrate my happy mood - a melodious song.

It's how we associate feelings with life. With tiny pleasures. Come to think of it, there's always a reason for us to do so. Knowingly or unknowingly, they always seem to work out in our favour.

Whether they are short-lived or whether they're entirely paced out, our tiny escapisms seem to be there for us, waiting at the curb side. There's always room to introduce new forms of such as well. The need to be present and willing to accept them is what helps change the situation.

The reason behind adding this as a driving force of life is to keep me occupied no matter what I think of myself.

We grab our cups of hot chocolate and stride onto the patio to sit on the swing. Ah, the swing, my old friend.

We carry a warm fuzzy blanket on our way there, since the air is chilly. We come by and situate ourselves on either end of the swing, placing our hot chocolates on the tiny table near me. She gets up and lights the fireplace to keep us warm. This is sublime, I think to myself. What a fabulous end to an eventful day.

I laugh to myself when I think of the nightcaps we had at the restaurant. Nothing will ever be as fabulous a nightcap as hot chocolate.

"How do you feel?" Her question takes me by surprise.

"How do I feel? Like in this moment, or generally?" I counter her.

"In general, at this moment, tell me how you feel," she responds.

"I feel liberated. Free. I think that's the best way I can put it." I reply.

"Free! What a delight!" she says. "I love feeling free. Why is free deemed to be something negative in today's world? There isn't any respect given to it."

"I really do not know. I think a lot of people have truly never lived, mainly because of the bars and the conditions that today's modern society has dawned on us."

"I guess so," she replies but loses what she was going to say. She has a confused look, but I can't figure out why.

"I don't think I've been this extricated from my routine life in a very long time. I mean, maybe I might have been neglecting myself and my own needs for a short time coming but at the same time, I really had no route to. Many aspects of my life were super demanding and required a great deal of time and patience." I go on, "Coming here may just have been the best decision I ever made in a while. Mainly because of how liberating this whole experience has been. I have tried and done things that I wouldn't dream of, back home! Sometimes I think that it may be the place, but I genuinely would like to believe that it's us and our mindset."

"I understand where you're coming from, I feel the same way too. Having lived here my whole life, I have been exposed to a lot of experiences. Both positive and negative, but it was the company which I kept that truly made the whole experience so worthwhile. Always! Whether it's being in a comfortable situation or doing something risky, I always have the courage to follow through with them, only because of the people I'm around," she continues to say.

"That has a lot of truth to what you're saying, I whole heartedly agree with you. I guess sometimes we just tend to lose focus on what truly matters. For example, I never knew I wanted to travel to *Serbia* until I just woke up one day and decided that I had enough of not wanting to take care of my own needs and went ahead straight out to book myself a ticket and got out of the country for some very well needed travelling." I express myself to her, "I knew that at the end of the day, regardless of what I said or did, I needed to take control of the situation and help myself be the best version of myself."

She smiled as she listened to me, she looked into the sky for a while and took sips of her hot chocolate when she just popped up a question. "Let us go on a long road drive tomorrow?"

I am truly caught by surprise, but this is a great surprise, the kind where your heart skips a beat but you know it's good. I respond back without thinking twice, "Yes!!!"

"Let's pack our bags for two nights and set out first thing in the morning tomorrow?" she asks.

"Sounds like a plan! I can't believe this is happening!" I say ecstatically.

"Me either! I don't know why or how, but I genuinely think this definitely calls for a road trip. A lot of girl time, an adventure of a lifetime! And honestly, with the way life has been going for the last two days, I think it would be crazy not to go!" she says.

"You're right! This seems so dream like to me. Pinch me! I genuinely am so excited at this moment. Maybe too excited, but this just feels so right, you know?" I respond.

"It's a crazy idea! But so crazily good!" she says.

"Okay, so where are we going?" I asked her excitedly.

"Let us head to the countryside! The weather is cooler and there are a lot more activities to do! We can probably ski as well if you'd like. I know a ski chalet there that has the cosiest cabins to offer." She says, "it would be like Christmas time, lots of mulled wine, ski gear, snow!!!"

"I have never once seen real snow, let alone ski!" I laugh out loud as I tell her.

"All the more reason to! We could get you a ski instructor for half a day. You'll be a pro after that! I myself learned to ski in half a day. It's super fun!" she says.

"Wow! I am so ready for this! But I wonder if the winter clothes I brought with me would be enough for the snow region." I respond.

"Don't be silly, you have my wardrobe to raid! Pick whatever you'd like. I have all sorts of cashmere, wool, fleece, you name it, I've got it!" she insists.

"No, I couldn't! I feel like I have been imposing way too much. I don't want to put you out." I respond.

"What! Nonsense! I have been imposing. Staying here while you are a guest at this mansion. And you've paid a great deal for it as well!" she says.

"No, no, absolutely not. Without you, I'm not sure I would be having such a brilliant time. Thank you, I mean it from the bottom of my heart. I genuinely have been through a journey of self-discovery in the past few days of my being here." My eyes swell up with tears because of the regret of never taking time for myself. Thank you for opening up your heart and home to me. I will forever be grateful for everything you're doing for me. It is helping me in ways that nobody, but only I can imagine. Thank you. Thank you so much.

Chapter  15

> *"Life is built not through experiences had,*
> *but through people we share these experiences with."*

"I'M SEVERELY OBLIGED. I mean it. Thank you so much." I respond, "So, when exactly do we leave and when do I start packing?"

"I was thinking maybe sometime early tomorrow morning? Let's leave as early as we can, to reach there at a reasonable time?" She says.

"Perfect! Makes more sense as well that way. We can head out super early and catch the best views!" I respond.

We soon retire for the night as we make our way upstairs to the bedroom nooks of the house. She heads into hers and I head into mine. Before each of us shuts our bedroom doors, we look back at each other and smile. Our smiles have something very familiar about them. There definitely is a level of familiarity between us, not considering the past few days that we've been spending together, but the level of familiarity just seems like it has been there for a long time. Long enough for us to realize that this is where the two of us actually belong in this moment. She nods her head as she shuts the door behind her. I soon shut mine as well.

I walk over to my room and run myself a hot bath to wash this day off. I want to be immersed entirely in this day, but I also know better than to not get into comfy clothes because of how tiresome this day has been. It has consumed my energy wholeheartedly and won't ask for more, because I have none to spare!

I walk over to the washroom and run the tap of hot water as I pour myself some of my rose salts to soothe the water more than it already will. I walk over to the record player and situate a lovely record by *Aretha* as I step into the tub to soak this delightful day off.

The candles are lit, the music is serene and the ambiance is just perfect to have me well-rested before we go about countryside tomorrow. I step into a symphony of tunes as I plan out my day for tomorrow. I have the basic necessities for my winter attire but she's promised to lend me some, should I fall short of any.

I step out and blow off the candles and switch them out on my dim nightstand. I open up the wardrobe and I lay out all my clothes that I have been somewhat prepared for my wintery travels this time. A cashmere sweater, a woollen muffler, a pair of my leather high-knee boots and a few knitted pieces are what seem to come out of my travel bag. I think to myself just how lucky I am to have everything at my disposal at this very point in time. I know for a fact that I can ask her for whatever piece of clothing I need right now and she would have it for sure.

That mighty large wardrobe of hers sure does hold wonders in the forms of different fabrics, for sure.

I draw my curtains to let in the night breeze, it browses past me and I feel chills. The good kind of chills that send you down a lovely spell, the kind that makes you appreciate everything, the kind that can't help but make you wonder just how heavenly everything seems right about now.

Accepting this for whatever it has come down to be, will be the best decision I will ever make for myself in my life, I just know it.

I smile as I look at the moonshine on the trees, glistening with the faint breeze in the back.

I walk over to my bed as I take off my fuzzy slippers and undo my silk robe, then tuck myself into bed as I dream of how beautiful tomorrow will be.

I wake up and I'm greeted by the gentle zephyr and warm radiance of sunshine outside. I know this, feels like déjàvu.

I laugh to myself as I put on my robe and strut downstairs.

"Top of the morning, isn't it?!" she announces before she even sees me, expecting my arrival.

"Certainly! How'd you sleep?" I asked excitedly.

"Well, darling, thanks! I'm so looking forward to today's trip that I slept off excited and woke up elated!" she gushes.

"There's no way! Me as well! I barely got any sleep just thinking of how amazing today will be! The memories I'm about to create. The laughs I'm going to have, the wind I'm going to feel graze my skin. I don't want to get too excited but please know that I don't think I've ever been this invested in a trip! Even more than I was before when my solo trip was planned for!" I rant animatedly.

"I am too! I've been but this feels like the first time! I'm excited like never before. Let's gather our stuff and get ready to leave?" she asks.

"Absolutely! I'll shower and make us some coffee!" I announce.

"Coffee on me, you go shower and get dressed," she insists.

"Yes ma'am!" I give in and quickly head upstairs to get dressed and pack my stuff.

"Darling! Hold on please!" I hear her call out to me as she ascends to my room.

She enters the room and finds me by the side of my bed, packing, with all my stuff sprawled across the bed. "Sorry for the mess, just arranging what to take and whatnot to."

"Oh, sweetie," she chuckles and goes on to say, "I've played out all my winter clothes, come find them in my room. Pick whatever you like and keep it. I have far too many and I'd like you to have whatever you like!"

"How kind! You've made me an offer that I know I won't be able to resist!" I gush.

"All right, then come on over to my room!" she says.

Chapter

> *"We often get caught up in the daily struggle called life. Be like a child, see the magic in everything around you."*

WE WALK TOWARDS her room and the second I open the door; my eyes are greeted by the heavenly display of cashmere galore! There are lots and lots of *Vivienne Westwood* pieces that catch my attention almost instantly! I even spotted a few *Moncler* puffer jackets. Wow, a winter collection so exquisite. It put my measly winter stuff and other knitted pieces to such shame.

"This is fabulous! How is your collection so sublime? I never knew winter clothes would ever turn out to be so fashionable! I always thought them out to be oversized brooding clothes that just covered the fabulous clothes beneath!" I exclaim.

"These are years in the making. There are a bunch of these clothes that are rare vintage finds that my daughter and I would go out every weekend shopping for! We love vintage pieces. Things that have history. Every piece of my clothing here has a story of its own to tell. Come find them, which one would you like to take, darling?"

I flick through the clothes and eventually fall in love with 5 singular pieces. A lovely woollen scarf, two cashmere sweaters and a pair of corduroy trousers to keep.

I quickly scutter and bring all my pieces together and have them placed in my bag, ready to leave.

After a quick shower, I get into my fresh set of clothes and pair them with the trench coat that I came in wearing. And head downstairs. She's waiting there with her bags and two cups of coffee to go!

"Excited?" she asks.

"More than I've ever been!" I reply instantly.

We make our way to the garage and *Anna* passes over the car keys to me. I start up the Toyota Fortuner and get the car up and running!

I load our bags in the boot of the car and hop on over to the front side.

We soon head out to the main street. We are greeted by a few of the neighbours as they head out on their morning strolls. We smile and quickly drive past them.

I start up the sound system and get the car's heaters running.

"It's wintry outside today, isn't it?" she asks.

"Quite chilly! I'm not used to weather of this kind at all. My life has mostly been spent in hot sunny regions. Regions where I'm only exposed to cold air when the air conditioning is on!" We laugh together as I drive on.

As I drive, based on the directions passed on to me by the GPS system, I find myself in one of those many abstractions that I've been in since my arrival to this country.

Again, on the road in a foreign land, with no sense of direction, besides the one leading me to, I think to myself just how astonishingly crazy life is on its way. Given the way, we somewhat rely on others to make our way. The scenic view is beyond amazing. I just find myself gazing into this perplexing view that has presented itself to me. The green fields of grass extend out to the sun's horizon, just heaps and heaps of green land sprawled across with no end to its bounds. There are cattle grazing on the grass as well. I can't help but wonder just how I would ever get an opportunity to view this again.

Had I not been scrolling through the rental website when I initially booked the mansion, had she not had a plumbing issue at her place and had I not been receptive to let her stay in the mansion along with me, none of this would've happened. I would not be in this position. Driving this car up to the countryside and getting myself to explore such a wondrous scenic view with her guiding me by the side- there seems to be a familiarity with this situation once again.

The journey up to the countryside isn't too long a stretch. A total of around 5 hours and we reach our lodge. There were plenty of scenic views that we accumulated across our journey there. We stopped to gather ourselves some coffee along the way but not too many halts.

I get the car to a halt as we arrive at *Kopaonik,* the lodge we're staying at and step out. We're greeted by the staff as they quickly escort us to our lodging.

I enter the lodge and I'm completely enchanted by its view. It's mesmerizing in its way. It almost feels like a slice - very much out of this world. The entire lodge is blanketed by snow, which creates the most picturesque view. I am enthralled to be in this position, witnessing this magnificent view. It is nothing short of a grand painting.

At the foot of the lodge door, there's a basket with my name on it. Instantly captivated by this, though I can't help but wonder why there isn't a second basket or one with her name on it, I pick it up to look through its contents!

To our delight, we find a bottle of mulled wine, gingerbread cookies, some skincare products and two pairs of sleeping masks.

"What a lovely gesture! This is so kind. I love how welcome they make their guests feel," she says.

"Right? Reminds me of my host at the mansion that I'm staying at!" I quip.

"You are too kind, darling! Thank you, I'm flattered, to say the least," she says.

We get our bags in and place them on the stands.

The room is cosy, inviting. That's the best way I can put it. Imagine a room with heavy, rich wooden panelling and white carpeting in certain nooks to create a softer feel as opposed to the tough wood the exterior possesses. There's dim lighting that sets the tonality of the wooden interiors, causing the most perfect nuances with the layout of the lodge.

We situate ourselves on the couch as we deduce our travels. We both are exhausted after having spent long hours of travelling. But knowing us, these 5 hours won't have a singular effect on how we function individually as we've known it to be.

We pull our boots out and get the puffer jackets ready! We decide to explore the grounds and register ourselves for the ski program that they host.

The snow is magical, to say the least, I almost throw myself on a heap of snow that has piled up to replicate a small hill. I am then joined by her. We lay down in the snow for a good amount of time, not saying anything, until I felt a cold graze of ice suddenly hit me all at once. I look up to see it's her. She laughed while I continued to have this dazed expression slapped on my face.

I realize she's provoking war. A snow war. If that's what she wants, she'll have it. I quickly brace myself as I run towards her with a fistful of snow, aiming to lunge it at her knee, I completely miss it as it goes way past her and she lets out a laugh. I'm then caught off guard as she lunges a few balls on me. We're now in the midst of a very intense round of snowball fights, which seems to be going in everyone's favour but mine. I can't believe how terrible my aim is! I genuinely thought it would be better than what I have!

We quickly relinquish our game as we run short of stamina. We lay in the snow for a bit and say nothing. Just in each other's presence. This moment seems entirely different from the ones I've been living. It's been so long since I played like a child with not a single worry in the world.

Sometimes we just get so caught up with daily life, we don't realize that we also need to engage the child within us at the same time. The existence of our happiness relates heavily to the satisfaction of keeping our child within us playful as the days go by.

All mothers across the world can most definitely relate to whatever I am to say here, because of the universal experience that we all face. Having to deal with mum guilt may almost always consume us when we alienate ourselves with certain endeavours. Whether it's us having to service our workplace needs, or our own needs, or other needs, we often resort to over delivering while neglecting our small pleasures.

Chapter  17

> *"Life is full of firsts. Firsts of fears, firsts of true joys.*
> *The way you choose to go about them,*
> *determine your seconds."*

I KNOW I am nearing the end of my trip and this will be a moment, I won't be able to live again. This has been a trip of many firsts for me.

My first ever decision for a solo trip.

My first time sharing a mansion with a stranger.

My first time kayaking.

My first time going to dinner with a group of girls I didn't know.

My first time in the snow.

My first time driving in a foreign land.

I'm shaken out of my frenzy of thoughts by a little snowball that comes flying on my foot. I can't make out who it is out to be, but I quickly straighten myself and look to the direction of where it came from, I notice a small figure, a few meters away, a young girl. She seems apologetic and almost on the verge of breaking into tears.

She seems severely distraught as she notices that the snowball landed on my foot. As I walk to her, she flinches. I stop dead in my tracks and yell out to her, "Don't worry, darling! I'm not mad. Please don't be scared. What's your name?"

"Anya," she stutters.

"Why, that's such a lovely name!" I say, gently. "Where are your parents?"

"They're here, they just left to go get my younger brother from the kiddy ski camp." She says, sounding more confident with each word.

"Okay! Are you sure you're fine, Anya? Can I get you something?" I ask her.

"Yes, I'm fine. I'm sorry I didn't mean to hit you with that snowball, I was aiming for the tree." She says it apologetically.

"No harm done, love," I respond warmly.

She looks like my daughter. I wonder. They're both in a similar age bracket and have a similar demeanour, as far as I can tell. Something about her reminds me of my daughter. I am suddenly reminded of her. I haven't spoken to her at all! During the entire trip, we have not had a single conversation.

I think of how ridiculous it is of me to not have reached out to her or my family back home this entire time.

Anya is soon joined by her family, her mother, father, her brother. What a beautiful family, I think to myself. A family happily in love.

She calls out to me from behind as I smile and wave over to the parents. The kids scurry over to get into another snowball fight and I laugh to myself; as I see that beautiful family play, laugh and fall around with each other. What a heart-warming sight!

You could travel halfway across the world, but families are the same everywhere. It doesn't necessarily have to mean biologically related families. We create our families wherever we go. Whether it's with a group of friends, or with people you're just acquainted with but enjoy the company of, whether you converse with them every minute of the day, or if you don't converse for days or months on end, you know that at the end of the day you will always find your way back to them regardless of it all. Families aren't formed, they are built. Just like how I have built mine here in this foreign land.

I have built it with *Seira*, *Nina*, *Ella*, *Noel* and *Zima*. They feel like home. What is home anyway? Four walls? Absolutely not. Home is where the heart is and a home is sometimes a person. *Seira* really does feel like home.

In this moment, I am reminded of nothing and nobody but my mother.

My sweet mother gave me endless nights of advice, of love, of care and I have had a fair share of moments when she lost her temper at me, but I knew it was the best she ever did. She gave me a life that I hold with great pride today. All my learning has come from her. She allowed me to mess up and why wouldn't she? I'm only human after all. She's human too and has always tried to learn from mistakes. Just like how her mother let her do.

I know life can be quite tricky, but I'd like to think that people make life tricky. One minute we're here, the next minute we're elsewhere. Where do we begin? Where do we end? Where do we stop?

This is how life works its magic on us. Magic exists, for sure; magic exists in little things. The tiny things are what make life worth living.

I'm here sprawled across the snow, making angels with her and I can think of no better way to spend my days out.

"Hey! You, okay?" she asks me as I'm shaken out of my little inner monologue.

"Yes, yes, all good! Just thinking about, you know, life," I respond with a smile.

"Life! I see. Life is happening, baby! Look around! **Stop thinking and start living!**" she says cheerfully as she pulls me into the small hill of snow.

We land merrily on that tiny hill and laugh as we do.

"All right, so do we ski first or would you like to check out the snow trail?" she asks.

"Ski, please! I'll get boots on rental, I don't think I'm equipped with that, plus the gear and a trainer too!" I laugh as I say.

"Let's go!" she laughs back.

We quickly make our way to the ski rentals and find a lovely set of girls who assist us with the boots. We're given a bunch of ski gear to rent out and get ourselves started with. As I step into my boots, I can't help but wonder how people manage to get into them so effortlessly. They're super heavy!

She looks as graceful as ever, even trying her boots on and then there's poor dishevelled me, struggling to even take two steps in those boots.

We're led outside by the girls and are introduced to the ski instructor. She's a skier, so it's not too difficult for her, but she insists on taking lessons to serve as moral support for me, which I think is sweet. Doing something out of no need or necessity but out of a pure willingness to help someone out is great, isn't it?

Her benevolence isn't even the best thing about her, she selflessly is there to help out every step of the way.

Chapter

> *"Art is the true essence of being. Art is how you feel when you live it all, happiness, sadness, despair, everything."*

THE SKI BASE is filled with people. People who professionally ski, people who almost look like they could professionally ski, but don't professionally ski. Girls in groups learning to ski, families skiing alongside each other, people falling butt down because they don't know how to ski and people not skiing but just there for the vibes.

The sun is shining and hits my skin with the tiniest bit of warmth. It's such a lovely day outside today, I think to myself. The whole atmosphere is perfect, just as if this day was made for us to ski!

Our instructor is introduced to us, his name is Alex and he seems to be a lovely young man. He welcomes us to the range that he thinks is best for me - the beginner's level. I ask her if she'd like to move up a few levels, given that she knows the basics quite well, but she stays put next to me. I think to myself just how lucky I am to have such a fantastic skiing partner.

Alex helps train me; he teaches me the first thing about skiing - balance. Balance is so important in this sport; I find myself heavily concentrating on trying to stay afoot on both my limbs, but I simply fail to do so. Only because it's so tricky!

I have been laughed at countless times by her and Alex, but I don't mind. This is a fun experience that I am wholeheartedly relishing. God knows I won't get these moments back once I'm home. One because of the lack of snow and two because of the lack of her.

We goof around and get serious too! I eventually get a hang of the basics and soon find myself carefully gliding through the baby hills of snow quite effortlessly. Alex and she cheer me on as I stride myself through these tiny hills in a graceful manner.

Alex later confides the faith he has in my skiing skills and I am left to master the art by my own.

As he leaves, I sit down on the snow and look around.

With hour's worth of travel, I haven't been tired for a split second since our arrival. I don't think I've been tired this entire trip! Life is funny in that way; it doesn't slow down for anyone and here I am wishing time would! Life has been nothing but a rollercoaster these past few days. So surreal in the best possible way. Especially because of how fast paced everything has been. Who knew that I would end up befriending my host and travelling across the country with her and falling butt down while skiing with her as well. It's all rather funny when you think of it.

As I'm dancing through my mind with these thoughts, I wonder just when I'm going to get back to the lodge and call my daughter! I truly miss her. I miss everyone back home, but I don't feel an urgent need to get back home. My days in *Serbia* are planned out so blissfully in the best possible manner. Having to deal with such a lovely set of people has opened my mind to a lot of happenings across the world. I know I am now fully receptive to new learnings in life because of this shared experience that I've had in a while. I have met people from all walks of life, of different genders, of different ages, all coming together to create the most harmonious presence of camaraderie.

Especially for *Seira*, I have a lot to take back with me when I go home, I know this for a fact because I have never truly felt like myself, as much as I have in these past few days. I think what I most desperately lacked these few months, the reason as to why I even needed to get on a flight out and visit a different country was simply because of the lack of self-actualization and self-discovery that I have done.

I used to be able to figure out and deduce my own needs, whenever I needed to, but of late, I felt as though I was rummaging through deep crevices of my existence, to just find a single answer. And why is that? Why is it that I needed to shift my pace from one country to another? This was a journey I knew I had to take for myself, by myself and just for myself. This was a journey that was written for me, in the pages of my fate and destiny.

Being here in this present moment has done nothing but help me reach and attain my goals much more quickly. I sometimes wonder, how lost we get in everyday life, that we almost forget to sit and just breathe. Sit and breathe! The most mundane, simple tasks of a human's existence. We get so caught up in today's fast-paced world, that we sometimes don't even stop and look. Stopping and looking now almost seems like a measly chore to some people, come to think of it, where this should never be the case. Having to stop means opening yourself up to new challenges, new hurdles, new lessons and new journals. It means that you are accepting of different situations in life where you are not just receptive, but also proactive to possibly make an active change in whatever you think might be lacking, regardless of its nature.

Chapter

> *"Ever so often, stop and stare at life happening. Watch yourself and find solace within it."*

THE FEELING OF being here hits me in the most perfect sense. I am ever so enchanted by these moments that keep passing me by. There is a level of faith I bestow in the present, that reciprocates to me enjoying my time here severely.

She walks over to me ever so gracefully and situates herself on the piece of rock next to me and smiles. "Hey, you doing well? I hope the snow hasn't made you feel ill. It happens sometimes when you aren't used to weather of this kind."

"No no, I'm doing perfectly well. Very well that I don't think, I've ever felt this wonderful in so long if I'm being honest." I respond with a smile. I realize just how concerned she is for me. Always so kind.

"If you say so! I'm glad you're doing well. Do you want to come join me for a coffee at the ski café?" she asks.

"Absolutely! But I doubt I'll be able to get up. I'm glued to the snow below and indeed, I'm too lazy to bring myself up to my two feet." I laugh as I respond.

"Up then!" She says as she pulls her hands out to assist me to get up. She does and I'm on my feet again. We collectively fit into a burst as I stand there.

As we walk towards the snow café, I can't help but notice the number of people at the ski chalet. It's just impressive. We're all here today on this day, with no sense of connection whatsoever, but enjoying this perfect day in the snow, with the sun blanketing us for a little toastiness to adjunct the chills in the best possible manner.

We walk up to the café and I'm mesmerized! It is the most beautiful placement of a café in the snow. It sits out on this ginormous wooden ledge that extends over to the end of the snow-like cliff, with wooden detailing to add on to the beauty of white that is the snow. I see multiple people sitting outside, enjoying their meals and chatting away. They all look so enthralled by the scenes; I can tell by the amazed looks on their faces. Very similar to mine. I smile to myself as I walk upstairs to meet the entrance of the café.

We are greeted by the hosts as they walk over to get us seated. I request the seating that's available outside. We are quickly escorted outside by the prompt host.

We sit down and are presented with the menu cards. I flip through it. Gee! Am I hungry after all that activity I got up to? We peruse through it and are equally delighted when we find roasted tomato rosemary soup! One of the first meals with her and one of my first meals in this country, I think to myself as we near the end of my trip. I know it's been a whirlwind, but I am at such ease and peace in this present moment in time and I couldn't be any happier about it.

We place our orders for the soup and we individually get our cups of coffee to go with as we soak in the brisk summer but wintry breeze. She places an order for a double espresso while I order for a cortado. What a brilliant combination, I think to myself, the coffees and us!

"How does it feel? Being here after never having experienced snow before?" she asks me curiously.

She puts on her pair of shades and her hair flows beautifully with the wind. Her silver hair paints the foreground and background perfectly. There's such a beautiful acceptance to it all and I can't help but notice how glorious she looks.

"I feel like I finally belong. I think that's the best way I can put it. I feel like I truly, entirely and wholly belong," I respond with such satisfaction that is noticeable, I am sure.

She smiles and puts her hand out to hold mine. I feel a tinge of electricity running through my body as she does. I don't understand why, but I just do. But it feels like the type of electric current that's just about right. I don't know what sort is supposed to feel that way, but I found a home in it at that moment.

We are soon presented with our cups as we indulge in the coffees that we had respectively ordered. The taste of the coffee, the spectacular views, the brilliant weather and having her by my side right now make me feel as though all is well in the world. I will never have any problems at this moment whatsoever.

The waiter then comes by with our tomato soup just as we finish up our cups of coffee. What brilliant timing, I think to myself. The service here is undeniably good.

I feel as though I find myself in another one of my inner thoughts, thinking about how every moment is so fleeting. From finishing my coffee to being presented with my soup, quite literally has it translating to every moment has to end, regardless of how long you would want it to last. I wonder how different acceptance would have to be for different individuals, with their own perceptions, when it comes down to it at the end of the day.

Chapter

> *"Today feels like no other.*
> *It will always feel like no other. Seize it."*

I'M PULLED out of my train of thought by her as she quickly grazes my hand and looks at me in hopes of taking a sip of my soup. I smile and accept. How brilliant is this soup! I inwardly think to myself, but nothing compares to what I had a couple of days ago made by her. We finish up our soups and get to clearing our bill as we notice a pair of women. Quite like us in ages and demeanour, if I'm allowed to say.

We look at them and look back at each other, we smile because we know we're both thinking the same thing. **Finding a home in each other.**

As we exit the café, we decide to stroll around and bask in the snow before heading to our lodge. We sit down and play in the snow, ski a tad bit more and eventually find ourselves making our way back to our room.

We enter our respective rooms and I take off all the ski gear; while doing so, I realize just how heavy the clothes are. No wonder I'm so exhausted, I think to myself. This is eventually realized in my wanting to soak off all my long excursions for the day.

I get down to it and run myself a hot shower, then quickly find myself getting sleepy and wanting to retire for the night. I wrap myself in the fleece robe given to us by the lodging and walk over to her room to check up on her.

I knock and she answers, "Come in, angel."

"Hey, how are you doing? I see you've resorted to the same measures that I did as well."

"I'm rather tired I won't lie. From travelling all day and then skiing, I think I'm getting old!" she laughs casually as she goes on.

"Rubbish! Age is just a number. And I wish I look half as amazing as you once I reach your age," I respond.

"So, you agree I'm old!" she counters me in a joking manner.

"Absolutely not. I'm just ever so fascinated by your beauty," I say. "What are we getting up to tomorrow by the way?" I add as an afterthought.

"Oh, great you asked, I was just going to suggest a train ride for us!" she squeals in excitement.

"A train ride?" I'm equally curious but oh so euphoric too.

"Yes! Let's take the *Mokra Gora* valley train ride!" she says.

"*Mokra Gora*?" I respond in confusion because quite honestly, I am.

"Yes! It's a beautiful train ride to the valley. You won't find one like this in a very long time. And you can't leave *Serbia* without having experienced this train ride," she says, nodding slowly.

"Absolutely. I certainly want to visit. Please don't be bothered by my initial apprehension. It wasn't toward the idea, just that it came in as very unexpected! Please let's go!" I declare.

"Perfect! Let's set out first thing tomorrow!"

It is getting quite late in the night. Suddenly, I feel an urge to ring my family back home. It's my deliberate decision to stay away from work and all other commitments during this trip. Now, I can't take it anymore. I ring my husband's mobile. I eagerly wait to hear a human voice on the other side. But to my dismay, my call is not answered. Then I realize that time in UAE, where my family is situated, is three hours ahead of me which means there is no chance of getting my call attended now, in these odd hours of midnight. Mom guilt comes rushing to me.

I turn around to see, she has been gazing at me. We hug each other and sit in silence for the next few moments. This entire trip has been a journey of self-discovery for me. I have done things I never knew I would ever be able to. Having to even continue them is what puts me far in life. I think just how blessed I am to have had someone to guide me through this foreign land and help me out when I knew nobody was here. Someone who took complete ownership of being not just a tour guide, but also a wonderful friend. I look at her while I continue to count my blessings for this trip and I notice a single tear fall from the side of her cheek. I want to ask her what's wrong, but I notice she quickly wipes away the tear and turns the other way, in hopes of me not noticing it. I don't want to probe, so I ignore it but also keep an eye out just in case.

I never know what to do in such situations, I think to myself.

Why is it that I always shy away from confrontational features of this sort? Understanding the nature of certain situations in life may not be too easy, but I try to make the best of my abilities in said situations. I wonder if my upbringing had anything to do with the nature of how I deal with these situations. Maybe I lived a partially rigid lifestyle that didn't allow me to test the best of human abilities when it comes down to consolation, if anything. Sometimes I find myself wondering just how this is a situation that even plays out because of the level of embarrassment I feel in this instance. I know I need to rectify this situation for the better. I know better than to ignore it.

We hug each other and say our goodnights as I step out of the room and walk towards mine.

Chapter

21

> *"Journeys to new places in life always shape us for the future."*

JUST AS I find myself back in my room, I realize the time and have a small fright. It's way past what I realized the time to be. I quickly set up my bed and fluffed up the duvet. I walk over to the vanity and get my skincare out. I find myself lathering a good amount of my *La Mer* cream and just stopping to stare at the person looking back at me, imitating my every move.

"Hi fabulous!" I call out loud to my reflection in the mirror.

Life has its funny way of showing you to take a breather. Life had its funny way of showing me mine. I was working long strenuous hours, not being able to devote any time to my daughter, my son or my husband, let alone time for myself. I knew this journey needed to happen to help me refocus, recentre and realign my goals. Be it short-term or long-term.

Eventually, short-term goals help aid your long-term goals.

I confess, the one short-term goal that I needed to achieve, was to be able to sit down and accept my thoughts and listen to what my body needed. My body was deprived of rest and what did I do? I took a trip out and gave it the rest, it didn't receive these past few months. Even with no rest, I know today, that if I'm happy, doing what I'm happy about, the rest all will just be external noise and will aid to nothing but rubbish. I know that, today I am in my best shape, my best form and my best mindset. And I credit this to nothing, but pure happiness that I have felt these past few days, in this foreign land, where nothing feels foreign.

There has always been a situation in life where I have not always been happy with whatever was presented to me. Humans are insatiable creatures, always wanting more than what is being offered.

Completely submerged in my thoughts, I put down the skincare and walk over to my bed pulling the covers over me to find some warmth in this lodging blanketed by snow. I peek my hand out and turn off the bedside night lamp while I do so.

I wake up soon, excited for the day that holds such a brilliant first experience for me again!

I quickly freshen up and realize a knock on my door.

I know it's her, so I yell out, "Please come in, I'm up and ready!"

She opens the door and I am revealed to by the beautiful yellow dress worn by her. She looks pretty impressive in it. Her hair is knotted up into a low bun, with gorgeous blue drop earrings to add beauty to them in the highest regard.

I am mesmerized by her style, it's so trendy but elegant at the same time. How does one even achieve that? I think to myself.

"Are you excited?" she enquires, making a cute hand gesture.

"Yes, most certainly! Ever since I've sat on a train!" I respond chirpily.

She has a laugh and then goes on to say, "Everything has been taken care of, we just need to leave within the next hour for us to make it on time as we have over 3 hours from here to reach the spot!"

"Absolutely and thank you so much, I truly appreciate your efforts. All of them. From feeding me such brilliant food to helping me get over my fear of water, from taking me down to experience snow and now to experience a train ride with scenic views. I am so appreciative of your efforts. Thank you," I can't seem to stop.

She doesn't say anything, but instead smiles and embraces me in a hug. I feel at ease almost instantly. This again, like before, feels like home.

I get dressed in next to no time. I've put on a pair of my light-washed blue jeans, a white cashmere jumper and my trusty brown trench coat, all paired with my boots.

We gather our belongings, do a quick check-out and make it out the door to be greeted by the staff and our car. We exchange our pleasantries and find ourselves headed to *Mokra Gora*.

Serbia's countryside is blessed with mind blowing scenic beauty and the road drive was just amazing.

We find ourselves stopping by taking a few intervals ever so often, in hopes of a sense of direction from the locals. The locals here are beyond comforting and accepting of the tourists around this city, which goes to show how welcoming the people of this land are.

We find ourselves laughing as we catch onto a few moments of me having difficulties of understanding the language. Though I find it a bit difficult to trace the route upon their instructions, I always find myself appreciative of one who proudly speaks out in their native language.

We arrive at *Mokra Gora* and are instantly captivated.

We reached *Drvengrad Bamboo Village*, yes everything here is wooden. We soon find ourselves fascinated to know that it was built for a movie by the famous film director, *Emir Kusturica* but was left as it is after the movie ended. I am instantly captivated by the presence of nature in this town. I have seen the world, at least a decent chunk of it - *Germany*, *Netherlands*, *Egypt*, *Thailand* to mention a few - but none have ever had me mesmerized to such an edge.

"Wow," she says, baffled to the core.

"Wow," I chime in, in equal bafflement.

We roamed around there, to see the wooden church, eat at the wooden restaurant and it was all nothing short of classy.

We soon find ourselves catching up to the station and being greeted by one of the attendees. The *Šargan Eight* tour is nothing less than what the *Orient Express* would offer. The station is beautifully carved and I notice the authentic features that it has, completely in awe of it all.

We are then introduced to the room of the train after we purchase the ticket, ready to board it and take it on for more than it has to offer at the end of the day. She joins me simultaneously and we take our seats. The train is a beauty.

"This is everything and beyond," she says as she takes her seat in front of me. "Everything and beyond," she emphasizes. The seating arrangement is perfect and there's a great deal of homeliness offered that puts travellers at ease.

Our curtains are drawn. Curiosity gets the best of me and I pull the strings back to reveal a view so spectacular that the two of us gasp together. The mesmerizing beauty of *Zlatibor* mountains is to die for.

I don't know how to put it in words, but all I have to say is how serene this place is! I don't think I will ever feel what I feel right now. There is not a singular possibility of it happening.

I shrug it off and look at her, she looks so calm and content. Her profile is rather similar to someone else's that I know of or knew of. I can't put my head around it, but I know what I'm reminded of in this moment.

Chapter

> *"Nature and our lives are interconnected.*
> *They are both receptive to nurturing for its growth."*

THE TRAIN STARTS and I hear a *choo*! The engine is traditional, which results in steam being let out in the air. I almost feel like I'm a student going to attend school at *Hogwarts*! She's my *Ron Weasley* and I'm *Harry Potter*. I laugh out loud just as I picture us in our wizarding robes. What a bizarre but funny thought! Given the old body that this train holds, the interior just adds on like a cherry on top of the cake! It is retro styled that entirely adds up to the nostalgic atmosphere that the train holds.

As the train moves along, we are greeted by views even better than what was offered in the first go. Because the train follows a route through the *Zlatibor* mountains, we soon progress to higher ground. We look by and find huge puffs of cotton candy, eerily similar to what a cloud would look like! Green grass sprawled across the land beneath, nature's gift.

Turns, *twists* and *tunnels* were just fabulous to say the very least.

I never knew a train ride would equate to giving me a great deal of happiness. She's here looking over the window, completely in awe of the earth we live in - the wooden houses, the green land, the blue sky, the white puffs, the steam being released in the air, syncing with the sky. Everything in the now is how it is supposed to be.

After a long and scenic journey of *Mokra Gora*, the train arrives back at the station and we get off. As I come down, I look back at the train and smile. I smile because of how this large old piece of locomotive has given me an experience of a lifetime, alongside her of course. What a journey this has been, revitalizing my mind, body and soul.

I thank her as we head back to the car, because quite truly, this entire journey has felt like a home away from home for me.

We drive back and the journey is quieter than any before. Partly because we know this will now soon be coming to an end.

I will be leaving soon. I won't be here anymore.

She won't have me here at her mansion anymore.

I'll soon be getting back to real life. A life with my family, my job and my responsibilities as a mother, daughter, sister, wife, friend and a super busy professional.

I wonder what she was thinking at this moment.

Chapter

> *"Change is constant, whether we choose to accept it, refute it, or embrace it."*

SHE DOZES OFF mid-way through driving and I turn the volume lower and pull the windows down, I need to feel this flurry of air consume me entirely. I am here today, I will be here today and nowhere else besides this moment, I'm living in by myself and for myself.

We soon arrive at the mansion and we're greeted by *Anna*. How is she here so late? It's nearly 11:00 PM. I think to myself.

The second I pull up in the driveway, *Seira* wakes up and smiles. She's a little upset at me as well.

"What! We're home! Why didn't you wake me up? I should not have slept. I wanted to keep you company!" she says in a rush.

"No please don't worry. We're home now and besides, I wanted you to get some rest in. I have kept you on your toes ever since my arrival. Please don't be upset!" I plead, almost.

"I know, darling. I'm upset because I wanted to spend time with you, because of how soon you're leaving. I don't want to miss a single moment with you," she says in a comforting manner.

"I understand, I'm sorry." I apologize because nobody has said this to me in a very long time. And this feeling of wanting to spend time with me all the time. It's a beautiful experience!

Anna greets me and escorts me to the house. She lugs out the suitcases from the car and I help her while she does so.

At the mansion, I find myself wondering just how soon time has flown by in this country.

From working for over 12 hours in a day, I am here, relishing these moments, enough to last me a lifetime.

Time doesn't ever stand still; we make it happen. Whether it's done consciously or unconsciously. We need to realize the intricate details that sum down to equivalating life for what it is, not for what it was or can be.

We make our way through the back entrance, because we followed the trail from the driveway. We wanted direct access to the kitchen and I had not even been at the back entrance as well.

We soon find ourselves in the kitchen, she puts on a kettle for some chamomile and offers me the same.

I gladly accept and we soon find ourselves in the tiny arrangement we have when it comes down to kitchen responsibilities. She as usual, fixes up the tea and I get the cups out for her to serve.

She takes the stool at the kitchen island and I find myself seated at the corner of the island.

"So, last few days here, huh," she says casually.

"I know! I can't believe how soon time has gone by!" I respond back while sipping on my tea.

"I was thinking, just to end your trip on the right note, I want to take you by *Drina House*."

"*Drina House?* What's that?" I question her.

"It's one of the most coveted places in the country. I don't want to give much away; it'll take some of the fun out! But trust me, it's a place like no other," she replies.

"Wow! I love the inclusivity of the ambiguity. When do we get to see the beauty?

"I was thinking tomorrow. We can make a day trip out of it!" she says.

"Absolutely. I'm looking forward to it tremendously!" I announce.

"Great! We'll set out first thing tomorrow morning," she says.

We just chat for a bit before the two of us decide to settle for sleep as we have an early start to next morning. We exchange our pleasantries and wish each other goodnight as we head down to our rooms.

I walk into my room and I instantly feel a cool breeze. I realize I've left my window open and I walk towards it to shut it a bit, given how piercingly cold it is. As I walk to it, I look outside and realize the moon is in its full form tonight. Its shining so bright, ever so bright.

The view is clandestine at best. The stars are all shining, vast fields meet my eyes until the greatest lengths. I can feel a lot but can't see any.

Chapter

> *"Sweet nothings or sweet somethings, they're all comforting."*

IN THIS MOMENT, I am reminded of my husband. Back home we live in a sky-rise building, with our balconies offering the best view of the city. We sometimes spend our time after work over there. Once we are both home after our long working hours, with the kids in bed, we find peace and quiet in the wee hours of the night, with a cup of tea in each of our hands, talking away and spending those precious moments with each other.

I miss him. I haven't spoken to him or my kids over the phone during my trip here. I quickly grab my phone and give him a ring.

He answers the phone and greets me. I feel instantly at ease upon hearing his voice. I feel very light in this moment and we converse for the next few minutes. I tell him about my trip and how lovely it has been with her. He feels equal excitement for me and wishes for me to be back home soon. He assures me that, the kids are doing well though they miss me. We converse for a few more minutes as we both decide to hit the sack.

I smile as we say our goodnights and head down to get some sleep.

The next morning, as usual, we catch the car outside and I drive ourselves to *Drina River House.*

I am clueless as to where we're even headed to and turn on the GPS. I realize the drive isn't too long and we just carry onto this place, *Bajina Bašta*. The journeys I've been on over this country is fabulous. The entire ride is peaceful at its best, we chat the entire time and appreciate the wondrous views that are offered on our way there.

We soon arrive at the spot and get ourselves situated afar, given the lack of parking spots.

I don't know where I'm being taken to, but I do know this has got to be one of the prettiest places I have ever been to! The surrounding nature captivates, bringing out the true essence of life.

We are near the water; I can hear the waves crashing by the shore and I smile internally. Once upon a time, these water bodies used to scare the life out of me, but today I want it to embrace me entirely.

"Come along! What do you think?" she says smiling over to me.

"This is nature at its best!" I say simply.

The view that meets my eyes!

The *Drina River* is flowing majestically, nestled between trees of all kinds and what surprises me the most is this little house. There's a house! On the river!

"How is this a thing? A house on a small rock in the middle of the river!" I ask her

The entire view defies nature and fascinates my eyes.

"Legendary! Thank you for showing me this place!" I exclaim.

We make our way closer to the house to admire its beauty and we find ourselves at the riverbank.

I sit down on a rock in the bank, with my legs grazing over the river water and I breathe in nothing but nature. I can't recollect the time when I was at this much peace with myself.

She sits next to me and starts narrating the story of a young boy and his friends who first built the little house in the middle of the *Drina River* several decades ago. I can sense the level of admiration in her eyes. Yes, she is narrating the history of the tenacious tiny house and the friendship between the boys. I listen with all my ears as she explains how the 'Serbs' rebuild it every time the river in its course or nature causes colossal damage to the tiny abode.

There really is no place like this. Being away from my family, but having found one here, makes life even more beautiful and worth living. The entire journey here has been fabulous and gives me the reassurance I needed, to keep seizing each day to the best of its offerings.

I notice other families at the *Drina River*, appreciating this scenic view like me. The sun is shining bright and I notice birds chirping along. This is life, life's best offerings right now by nature.

We spend a good amount of time here just taking it all in, sometimes in silence and sometimes chatting away.

We soon realize the time and decide to head back to the main city to catch up on dinner. Our drive back home is quiet again, mainly because we know today is gone and we won't get it back again. Knowing that I'm leaving is causing pain, to her and me both. We don't discuss it but instead listen to music and drive back to the mansion.

We arrive and go to bed directly, mainly because of how long this day has been. In hopes of a better tomorrow and more to come.

The next few days at the mansion are spent with her in the most beautiful way possible. We go out picking wild berries from the field adjacent to her mansion. Shopping at the local market is something we enjoy a lot.

Considering my eye for history and architecture, she takes me to the famous monuments like *Kalemegdan fortress, the Temple of St Sava* and *Studenica Monastery* to name a few. The grand beauty of the past stands still here!

At times we find ourselves exploring the nightlife in the city across the banks of River *Danube* and *Sava*. The rhythm and enthusiasm of meeting and spending time with a long-lost friend is what I feel then.

We enjoy every bit of people-watching while strolling through the streets of *Knez Mihailova*, full of cafes and shops exploring the *Slovic* and *Mediterranean* dishes.

On one fine morning, she takes me to *Novi Sad*, to explore the monasteries, synagogues and wineries there.

One day we go out to see the river and end up kayaking as well, meet the little family of ducks that just happen to be at the very same spot we discovered them.

We pick out fresh apples from the trees in her yard, paint together in her studio, in the garage. I must admit, *Art* is blended in her just like her beauty and her grace.

Basically, living life to the greatest of its capacities with zero regrets whatsoever. I feel alive in every single moment that passes by. Every breath almost revitalizes me tremendously. It is serene!

Chapter

25

"The most beautiful journey of all, the journey of life."

TOMORROW IS THE day I leave. We have decided not to roam around outside too much, but rather spend the whole day in the mansion. A lazy day, I wake up late. I am still in my cosy bed. The wind flowing in through the half-opened windows carry a familiar fragrance, but it is gone before I could identify it.

I don't want to leave; I think to myself. My days here have felt like self-discovery and have opened me up to a number of experiences I would never even have considered a few weeks ago. This has changed me for the better, I just know it. My family and friends back home will not be greeted by the previous version of me, but by a newer, reformed me.

I find myself packing away my belongings soon enough. It's the night before my morning flight to head back home. I have tiny knick knacks sprawled across the house, much like the glass birds that caught me off guard when I first arrived.

I am greeted by a knock on my door mid-way through packing my clothes.

She enters.

"Hey! How have you been? I didn't see much of you the entire day," I say.

"I'm good my angel, thank you. How are you? All set to go?" she enquires.

"All set, but not ready or willing to leave just yet," I respond with a laugh, but there's a sadness to my laugh. I think we both realize it, but nobody addresses it.

I am very good at hiding my emotions because of my rigid nature. Not because I choose to, but because of the way I am or have been conditioned to feel.

"I will miss you, angel." she says.

"Lord knows how much I'll miss you," I respond.

We just hugged each other at that moment, not caring about a thing in the world. Our moment is here and we choose to accept it for how it has come, nothing will stop it. Nothing can stop it.

We pull away and are both greeted by each other's tears. She's crying and I'm crying. We hug again now laughing and crying. This definitely is a bittersweet feeling. Bittersweet in the best regard I must say.

We don't say a word to each other, we just stand there, as if time has now stood still. Nothing in this moment matters.

She helps me pack away a few of my things, bringing in stuff from the washroom, from other rooms and from the grand salon. She effortlessly helps me pack away the past few days of me around this house.

"Hot chocolate? For old times' sake?" Persuasively she asks.

"I'd be crazy to decline a cup of hot cocoa!" I respond with equal persuasion.

"Come along then!" she says as she holds my hand and brings me down to the kitchen.

She brings the cocoa to a boil and I help with the arrangement of the cups. We soon find ourselves on the porch. On the swing all over again. We truly have come full circle. I laugh internally as I visualize my first night here.

"Thank you for coming here and staying with me. Life will truly never be the same now," she says looking up at me between sips of her cocoa.

"I second that! I have truly learned how to live and I have nobody to thank other than you. You have really opened me up to such beautiful journeys. The most beautiful journey of all, the journey of life," I say.

We just sit there in silence for a major part of the time. Not because we didn't have anything left to say, but because we just wanted to sit there in each other's silence, saying nothing but everything at the same time and just to feel at home.

We soon call it a night, she goes to her room and I go to mine. Just as I close my door, she knocks, just pulls me in for a hug, kisses my forehead and says, "I will always be here for you, angel. I'm not leaving, I promise."

I tear up all over again and thank her for everything she has done for me.

I soon get to my bed and pull the covers, shut the lamp off and stare out the window. The open window, with the white curtain breezing so elegantly with the night breeze, illuminated by the moonlight. I smile and thank myself for taking this trip out. I wouldn't be who I am today without that one booking on that one site, for this very mansion. Though I am happy and content, sleep didn't embrace me the whole night.

Chapter

"Nothing is ever the same".

I GET UP from my bed early the next morning and I'm greeted by *Anna*. She has brought me a cup of coffee to my bed. She draws my curtains and informs me that *Dejan*, the driver who got me here, will be at the mansion in an hour.

I thank her for the information shared and ask *Anna* where *she* is.

She is taken aback and questions me. "What do you mean, ma'am?"

"I am sorry, but what do YOU mean, by 'what do you mean,' *Anna*?" I respond with the tiniest level of annoyance. I repeat my question, "Where is *Seira?* The owner of this mansion? Your boss?"

"Ma'am, I have no clue what you're talking about. This is starting to scare me a little. The owner of this mansion is back in the US. It belongs to *Mr. Richmount* and his wife. Though they have many belongings left here, they visit here every two years only. I don't understand who you've confused him with and I am the caretaker, the only one who lives here."

I am in a state of shock. I don't understand what is happening right now at all. I politely ask *Anna* to leave the room and allow me a few minutes to get ready as *Dejan* would be arriving soon. I need time to digest what I just heard, but I don't have any as I am running late to reach the airport. I feel as my head is spinning.

I quickly pull out my laptop and look at my bookings, to find out the profile of the person with whom I had a conversation with, on the mansion's rental website.

I am shocked to find what *Anna* has said is true! I was conversing with *Mr. Richmount*, the entire time!

Who was *she* then? I am in a state of confusion and despair. Because of, what on earth has unfolded in the past few days?

I ignore these thoughts for a bit while I head into the shower and quickly get dressed to meet *Dejan* downstairs as he is taking me to the airport.

I say my goodbyes to *Anna* and thank her for everything as I make my way to *Dejan's* car.

"Miss! I hope your trip here has been a wondrous one!" *Dejan* says.

"Yes, *Dejan*, thank you! Good to see you!" I respond with a forced smile.

Dejan's car seats have changed, but his driving skills most certainly haven't.

With bumps and bruises along the way, we finally make it to the airport. He helps me lug out my suitcases and escorts me to the gate of the airport.

I thank him and just stand at the gate. I look back and say goodbye to this land one last time. There's a great deal of rush at the airport, people everywhere, but through that crowd, I notice a familiar face. It's *her*. WHAT! What on earth is she doing here?

I yell out to her and just look back to place my suitcases by the wall, but I no longer see her as I turn back to make my way towards her.

I don't understand what is happening and I fall into a state of great confusion. But I have no time to stand back and wrap my mind around this all.

I finish my check-in, rush to my gates because I'm late and I just make it on time, luckily. I take my seat and I'm greeted by the air hostess. She gives me a glass of water and I feel she notices the visible anguish on my face.

I thank her and prepare myself for takeoff.

I'm looking out the window when it hits me all at once. I can't believe what greets my eyes. As I look outside, I notice a series of clouds joined together, replicating my beloved mom's profile.

I am in a state of shock as this comes by. A vague profile of my mother's beautiful smile. My mother who passed away years ago.

I can't believe this. Not one bit.

As I sit there with my eyes closed, all those moments I have been experiencing for the past few days come back to me in a hurried gush. Realization dawns on me, slowly, that I have been hallucinating this entire time.

Overwhelmed, by a severe wave of emotions, my eyes welled up with tears.

The plane takes off and with it departing, my heavy emotional baggage departs as well. I sit there, thinking to myself, just how grateful I am to my mum for being here for me, time on end.

I close my eyes and find myself slipping away into a moment of tranquillity as I realize my mom has always been here for me, I hear her soft tender voice saying, "I am always there for you, my angel."

I take a deep sigh and smile to myself as I realize that *I'm here in this fleeting moment, nowhere else. Just here!*

When was the last time you stopped to listen to the wind blow through the trees? Or stopped to listen to a river as it flowed past you or the crickets and frogs and other living things as they make their music? When was the last time you listened--truly listened--to a favorite song, paying attention to the lyrics, the drums, the rhythm, the guitars or strings?

Tom Walsh

about the author

Dr. Sopna Nair is a Senior Structural Engineer and Lead Sustainability Consultant during the day and at night she enjoys penning down her thoughts and emotions in the form of stories.

She grew up in India, a country rich in art and culture and a decade ago moved to Abu Dhabi and found acceptance in this land for herself as well as her spouse, daughter and son.

She is passionate about books, so much so that she wrote the first of many.

Being a self-driven woman, she is devoted to giving back to the society, particularly to underprivileged women. Aside from her Engineering career, her lust for life is fuelled by travel, friends and dance.